MOTHERS'
INSTINCT

MOTHERS' INSTINCT

A NOVEL OF SUSPENSE

BARBARA ABEL

Translated from the French by Susan Pickford

HARPERVIA

An Imprint of HarperCollins*Publishers*

MOTHERS' INSTINCT. Copyright © 2012 by Fleuve Noir, département d'Univers Poche. All rights reserved. Printed in the United States of America. No part of this book may be used or reproduced in any manner whatsoever without written permission except in the case of brief quotations embodied in critical articles and reviews. For information, address HarperCollins Publishers, 195 Broadway, New York, NY 10007.

Translation copyright © 2023 by Susan Pickford.

HarperCollins books may be purchased for educational, business, or sales promotional use. For information, please email the Special Markets Department at SPsales@harpercollins.com.

Originally published as *Derrière la haine* in France in 2012 by Fleuve Noir, département d'Univers Poche.

FIRST HARPERVIA EDITION PUBLISHED IN 2023

Designed by Terry McGrath

Library of Congress Cataloging-in-Publication Data has been applied for.

ISBN 978-0-06-341468-6

24 25 26 27 28 LBC 5 4 3 2 1

A thousand thanks to Jean-Paul, whose help from the other side of the world was invaluable to me

PROLOGUE

Laetitia parallel-parked perfectly on the first try. Unfortunately, this did little to improve her mood.

"The Nintendo goes off now, Milo, we're here," she said automatically.

The boy in the back seat barely raised his eyes from the screen.

Laetitia climbed out of the car with her briefcase, Milo's backpack, and two bags of groceries. Her hands full, she knocked on his window with her elbow to catch his attention.

"Come on, Milo, I've got all this stuff to carry!"

"Wait, let me just save the game!"

The bags were sawing at her fingers, and her son's laziness caused Laetitia's temper, already simmering, to boil over.

"Let's go!" she snapped. Her parking job was about the only thing that had gone right today. "Get out of the car now, or no Nintendo for the rest of the week!"

"Yeah, OK!" He sighed, still glued to the game. He slid over to the edge of the seat, set one foot on the sidewalk, and dragged himself out of the car like a dead weight.

"And shut the door, if it's not too much to ask!"

"Laetitia!" She froze when she heard the unexpected voice. "Do you have a moment?"

She turned around. Behind her stood Tiphaine, panting in her running gear. A sheen of sweat covered her face, her bangs plastered to her forehead. When she got no response from Laetitia, Tiphaine went over to Milo and ruffled his hair.

"You doing OK, big guy?" she said kindly.

"Hi, Auntiphaine!" he beamed.

Laetitia strode over angrily, grabbed her son's arm, and pulled him behind her.

"Don't you *dare* talk to him!" she hissed.

Tiphaine barely flinched. "Laetitia, please, can we at least talk?"

"Get inside, Milo!" Laetitia ordered.

"But Mom . . ."

"Now!" Her tone told him not to push his luck. After a moment's hesitation, Milo went inside, pouting.

Laetitia turned back to Tiphaine. "Now you listen to me, you crazy bitch. If I see you anywhere near my son again, I'll scratch your eyes out."

"Listen, Laetitia, can't you understand that I never wanted . . ."

"Shut your mouth!" Laetitia hissed, eyes screwed tight in an exasperated scowl. "Keep your pathetic excuses to yourself. I don't believe you in the slightest!"

"Really? What *do* you believe, then?"

Laetitia gave her a look of utter scorn.

"I know *exactly* what the hell you're trying to do, Tiphaine.

But I warn you, if anything—*anything*—happens to my son, I'll call the cops on you."

Tiphaine seemed truly taken aback. She stared questioningly at Laetitia, trying to figure out what she meant. Then, as if suddenly realizing nothing would change Laetitia's mind, she sighed, not trying to hide how Laetitia's attitude pained her.

"I don't know what crazy thoughts have got into your head, Laetitia, but I promise you one thing: you're wrong. Please, just try to believe me. Not for my sake, but for Milo's. Because you're destroying him, bit by bit."

Laetitia arched one eyebrow, a look of contempt on her face. A cruel gleam flashed in her eyes like a lightning bolt in a stormy sky.

"Well, I guess you *do* know all about destroying children," she shot back, her voice almost silky.

Laetitia didn't see the slap coming. As the word *children* left her lips, Tiphaine struck her across the cheek. Laetitia stood stunned for a moment, eyes wide with shock. The groceries and bags sawing at her fingers seemed to weigh several tons. She dropped them to raise one hand to her cheek.

"How *dare* you!" Tiphaine raged, choking back tears, as if to justify the slap.

The two women stared at each other for a moment, sizing each other up, the air crackling with hatred. A voice rang out, interrupting the fight before it started.

"Laetitia!"

A man rushed out of the house Milo had just gone into. David grabbed Laetitia by the shoulders and pushed her behind him protectively.

"She hit me!" she blurted, still in shock.

"B-but some words hurt worse," Tiphaine stammered, aghast at the turn the confrontation had taken.

David gave her a withering stare, weighing his words carefully as he pointed at her with a threatening finger.

"You've gone too far this time, Tiphaine. We'll be reporting this."

Tiphaine gritted her teeth, barely concealing the storm of emotions raging inside her. It took her a few seconds to master herself. Choking back her sobs, she nodded.

"Fine, David. You do that. You see, the big difference between us now is that I have nothing left to lose."

David gathered up the groceries spilled across the sidewalk and pulled Laetitia inside, slamming the door behind them. Tiphaine stayed put, trembling all over, until she felt calm enough to walk back down the same path to her side of the duplex. She pulled the keys from her pocket, opened her own front door, and stepped inside.

CHAPTER 1

Seven years earlier

"Cheers!"

The three of them clinked their glasses—two champagne flutes and one glass of water—in a celebratory toast. There were sudden giggles, knowing looks, nods, and loving smiles. David and Sylvain sipped their champagne, savoring the prickling of the tiny bubbles. Laetitia put down her glass of water and stroked her boldly swelling belly.

"Not a drop of alcohol since you found out, then?" asked Sylvain.

"Not a single drop!" Laetitia said proudly.

"My wife is a saint," David lovingly teased her. "You can't imagine what she's putting herself through to give our son the best start in life. Zero alcohol, zero salt, zero fat, low sugar, steamed vegetables, fruit all day long, fish instead of red meat, yoga, swimming, classical music, early nights . . ."

He sighed. "The past six months have been *so boring*!"

"I'm not a saint, I'm *pregnant*, dummy!" Laetitia playfully smacked her husband on the thigh.

"And she keeps going on about parenting rules . . . poor kid! This mom will run a tight ship, let me tell you."

"You guys are already talking about parenting rules?" Sylvain looked surprised.

"Of course!" Laetitia said, suddenly serious. "Best time to do it is right now. When you're facing the problem, it's already too late."

"What sort of things are you discussing, then?"

"All sorts. Back each other up, don't undermine each other when the kid is listening, no sweets before they turn three, no Coke before they're six, no Nintendo before they're ten . . ."

Sylvain whistled, impressed. "We'll tell him that if you guys are too strict, he can always come over to us!"

David glanced at his watch.

"We should have waited for Tiphaine before raising a toast," he said. "She'll be annoyed she missed it."

"Not a problem. First off, she hates champagne, and anyway, she didn't want to stress herself out and keep us waiting. She's . . . kind of tired these days."

"Well, what's the champagne for, then?" Laetitia asked. "A nice bottle of wine would have been fine, you know."

The question caught Sylvain unprepared. Casting around for a plausible reason, he sputtered, "Well, because, you know . . ."

"I *don't* know," Laetitia said, laughing at his obvious discomfort. But then she realized there was only one reason to open a bottle of champagne: good news. She studied Sylvain for a moment, sure he was hiding a secret, eager to tease it out of him. Then the lightbulb went off.

"She's pregnant!" she cried, bolting up straight in her armchair.

"H-huh?" stammered Sylvain, looking even more ill at ease.

"Are you two expecting too?" David asked, beaming in delight.

"No!" exclaimed Sylvain. "Well . . . I mean . . ."

The doorbell rang, saving him from their inevitable questions. Laetitia leaped to her feet and waddled to the hallway as fast as she could. "Congratulations!" she called out, vanishing down the corridor.

"Please don't say anything!" Sylvain begged. "She made me *swear* I would wait!"

He turned to David, a look of comical dismay on his face. "She is going to *kill* me!"

David burst out laughing and got up to kiss his friend on both cheeks.

"Welcome to the club! How far along is she?"

"Three months."

Laetitia opened the front door, her whole face lit up with happiness.

"Darling!" she cried, her voice filled with laughter. "Our children will grow up together! Isn't it wonderful!"

Without waiting for Tiphaine's response, she pulled her in for a long hug.

CHAPTER 2

Later, when they looked back on that evening, the first thing David recalled was the perfection of each moment—the incredible joy in each glance, each gesture, each word. Their future plans, their promises and laughter, and the feeling of coming home to a family—one he had chosen for himself rather than been dumped into—gave him the sense of connection he had so longed for as a child cut off from his roots. An unwanted orphan, passed from foster families to children's homes, he had climbed a steep, rocky path to adulthood, walking the delicate tightrope between good and evil, nearly falling off a hundred times and clinging on a hundred times more. Until he fell off for good. Prison. And then a chance for a do-over.

Back to square one.

His own square one was right here. Laetitia. And the tiny frog-like creature in her belly. His very own little munchkin. The son he would give everything he had missed out on, whose hand he would hold to keep him on the best path. He always said "best path," not "right path," because as far as he could see, the "right path" didn't exist: it was a trap, a mirage, a lie told to children to keep them on the straight and narrow. Keep your head down. Don't draw attention to yourself. Just keep walking, head down. Don't glance sideways.

What a joke!

Real life isn't about straight lines. Life is one vast expanse of rugged terrain, riddled with obstacles, twists and turns, and deviations. A maze full of pitfalls with no straight lines in sight. The shortest path between two points is the one you know best.

But whatever you do, whatever milestones you pass on the way, at the end of the road you'll always end up in the same place.

That's what David thought. Before he met Laetitia.

He had done what everybody does. He took the only path open to him—a rope bridge across a chasm, without a map or a handrail. Without the two guides who should have been there to shepherd him patiently and lovingly into adulthood.

So he fell.

He started out with petty crime. Pot at thirteen, coke at fifteen, barely into puberty and already chasing cash—small-time dealing, the wrong crowd. He was caught up in the machine. Petty crime turned into burglary, breaking and entering, aggravated assault.

Two years in juvie.

Once he was out, he attempted for the first time to climb back onto the bridge. To keep moving forward. David clung to what help he could, but not much was there—just a few strands of rotten rope that snapped under his fingers and broken boards that crumbled away beneath his feet. It was a slippery slope, and he fell back down. Four more years inside, with the men this time, for armed robbery.

On his second release from prison, he made himself a promise. He would *never* go back. He pulled himself back up onto the bridge. He kept going, whatever the cost. At first, he crawled on hands and knees, washing dishes in a Chinese restaurant to pay for a single attic room. Three hundred euros a month, no hot water or heat, a shared bathroom on the landing, cockroaches scuttling across the walls. Then he shuffled on his knees, driving a bus to pay for a slightly larger room with hot water and heat—still no toilets, but at least no more cockroaches. And then gradually, he managed to stand, carefully testing his balance at every step, one foot in front of the other, taking it slowly. It took him several years.

By twenty-seven, he was a hospital janitor and able to rent a studio apartment with its own bathroom.

That's where he met Laetitia. At the hospital, that is, not in his studio or bathroom.

Her own journey had been a smooth, wide, fast road with no cracks or potholes, which wound through a lush green rural landscape: a scattering of fruit trees, a few low hills, and fields and meadows as far as the eye could see. A clear, distant horizon. Until her own two guides were knocked down by a truck.

It happened one night, as Sunday turned into Monday. And one wrong turn was all it took. Her parents were on their way home from an evening with friends, not too late, barely midnight. A smooth, wide, fast road. It was raining, though that hardly mattered. The story itself hardly mattered; it was just another accident. Wrong place, wrong time. Killed by what Laetitia later always called the three TRs: a truck, traumatic injury, and tragedy.

Her mother was killed on the spot. The car flipped, and she was thrown out and landed in the neighboring field, where she died. Her father lingered on for a week, hovering between life and death. Laetitia barely left his bedside, snatching a few hours here and there to sneak home and sleep, shower, change clothes.

And to meet David.

It was love at first sight. She was sitting in the corridor while her father was in the operating room, and though her face was etched with grief, her eyes red with weeping, and her nose raw from being dabbed with tissues, David could not help but find her touching and ravishingly beautiful. He felt an irrepressible urge to reach out and help her through the ordeal, and maybe, to walk with her a little way on her bereavement journey.

The following months were a strange experience for Laetitia. The fathomless pain of losing her parents waged a merciless battle with the giddy joy of falling deeply in love. She was an only child: the sole family she had left were a distant uncle and two cousins she had not seen since childhood. She grasped the hand David held out to her like a life raft in the middle of the ocean. At first, she did not know where it would lead, and she felt corrosive guilt about wanting the man she met at her dying father's bedside, daydreaming about him rather than mourning her parents. She'd catch herself smiling, fantasizing . . . and yet also blaming him for being there, as if he had come to turn her away from her grief. Hating him for something that was so good for her.

A one-way street. Deviations and detours. It took them

some time to find their footing and move forward—or at least try—together.

Eighteen months later, they moved into Laetitia's parents' house, her childhood home. She could not face the idea of selling it or renting it out. She could not picture strangers taking ownership of the walls that held so many of her memories and her family story. And now that she, like David, had no family, they decided to build a new one of their very own.

David had absolute faith in this new start. A second chance. They were on the best path, no question. Together they would conquer mountains, hand in hand. It would be a wonderful journey. For the first time in forever, David felt serene about the future. But he was forgetting one detail.

Whatever you do, whatever milestones you pass on the way, at the end of the road you'll always end up in the same place.

CHAPTER 3

David and Laetitia Brunelle soon met their new neighbors, Tiphaine and Sylvain Geniot. They were all around the same age, in their early thirties, easygoing, and their houses were separated by only a hedge. David found out that Sylvain listened to the same music as he did—King Crimson, Pink Floyd, Archive—and Laetitia saved Tiphaine from a kitchen disaster when she ran out of olive oil one evening. Tiphaine came by the next morning to return the borrowed bottle of cold-pressed extra virgin oil and Laetitia offered her coffee. Tiphaine gratefully accepted. It was the first of many coffees in what became a morning ritual that neither would miss for the world.

The two couples were cautious around each other for a few weeks, not wanting to get involved too quickly, but soon became firm friends.

The twin houses were identical inside and out. Each white-painted façade looked out over the street, with a varnished wooden door, a large downstairs window and two narrower ones upstairs, and a steeply sloping roof with a dormer window and a chimney that was purely ornamental. Behind each house was a terrace leading to a narrow yard, almost sixty feet long. The Brunelles had a plain lawn, which David mowed from time to time. In the Geniots' yard, Tiphaine, an avid gardener who worked at the local plant nursery, had laid out large flower beds overflowing with sweet-scented flowers, climbing plants, and shrubs and bushes, filling the space with color and fragrance all year round. There was even a small vegetable patch at the far end of the yard, Tiphaine's pride and joy.

Within a few months, the two couples were inseparable. More than just neighbors, they were the very best of friends. It was so easy to drop in for a few minutes or spend the evening together over a meal, drinking and laughing, sharing their thoughts, listening to music, and talking about anything and everything.

When Laetitia and Tiphaine got pregnant three months apart, it felt perfect.

Milo Brunelle made his appearance late one Tuesday afternoon, setting off a tidal wave of emotions in his parents' hearts and lives. Tiphaine and Sylvain came by to admire the newborn the very next day. Laetitia held the infant out to her friend, who held him carefully, as if he were made of spun glass.

"He's so tiny!"

Tiphaine nestled him on her own growing bump. The baby inside, still three months away from his own grand entrance, instantly reacted to Milo's presence, as if trying to reach out to the new friend who would be more than a brother to him.

Then it was Maxime Geniot's turn, early one morning after thirteen hours of labor. Thirteen hours of grinding pain that tore Tiphaine's body apart and futile screaming that did little to ease the agony, which grew worse by the second: *"I can't do this anymore! Please, make it stop!"* Swearing she would never do it again, that there would be no more children.

The baby came with the rising sun. Mother and father both fell silent, collecting themselves. They were choked with joyful emotion, and unable to tear their eyes away from the child.

It was an exhausting day. The families on each side rushed to the hospital as soon as Sylvain called, eager to be the first to see the new baby. Their parents, brothers and sisters, in-laws, nieces and nephews, all thronged around Tiphaine's bed, showering her with advice, comments, and compliments.

David and Laetitia hung back. They asked after Tiphaine by phone, saving their visit to the tiny hospital room to admire the new baby for the next day.

They were true friends.

And they knew what it was like, from recent experience.

That same evening, David and Sylvain left their wives snuggling with their new babies—one at home, the other at the hospital—and went out on a bar crawl. They drank to Maxime, to Milo, their wives, their friendship, to the future, and while they were at it, they drank to the whole world, the fine weather on its way, the wonderful fathers they knew they would be. They drank and talked, long and hard.

Was it the beer, the exhaustion, the overspill of emotion? Sylvain began to pour out his innermost thoughts to David about coupledom, families, the best way to bring up children, how he would handle Maxime. He saw his own role as a father as one of crucial importance. He would always be there, looking after his boy, ready to listen with an understanding ear, not like his own father, who did nothing but complain all the time: kids, noise, music, fast food, video games, friends from school . . . life! The man was just miserable, through and through. And a terrible communicator, unable to give a straight opinion without criticizing. Everything was better before, his father claimed. When he was young.

"When he was a young man, it was the same as today, just more goddamn *boring*!" Sylvain slurred.

"Do you get along with him now?" David asked. His own parents were still a touchy subject: he often thought of them, especially now that Milo had come along, showing him how fragile, vulnerable, and defenseless babies were.

The question had come back to him time and time again, haunting him ever since Milo's arrival. How could any parent abandon their own child?

Unaware of his friend's distress, Sylvain shrugged, staring into the distance.

"I've given up on a close father-son bond, he's given up on having a perfect son. We get along OK. No complaints."

David nodded pensively. He was also striving to be the best father he could, though unlike Sylvain, he had no one to compare himself to.

They sat in silence for a moment. Then, realizing they were sinking into an abyss of morose thoughts, David bought two more beers and changed the subject.

"So, how did you and Tiphaine meet? You've never really said . . ."

The question caught Sylvain off guard. He stared at David

in surprise for a few moments, as if he had said something shockingly indecent.

"It's not a nice story," he muttered.

"What?"

David thought he had misheard. He began laughing, confused yet intrigued, and stared at Sylvain to see if he was joking.

Sylvain stared darkly into his glass, swirling the coppery liquid as if a tragedy lay in its depths. Finally, he said softly, "Forget it."

David didn't press him further. Torn between the burning curiosity sparked by Sylvain's reaction and the sense of embarrassment that now hung in the air, he said nothing. The alcohol stretched out time, giving the situation a strange sense of unease and mutual incomprehension. Sylvain was stubbornly silent. David, increasingly uncomfortable, looked at his watch.

"Three in the morning! Time to head home . . ."

He stumbled out of his chair, leaning heavily on its back for support. He picked up the jacket slung over it and started wrestling it on.

"It was five years ago," mumbled Sylvain, who had not moved an inch. "Tiphaine worked at a drugstore back then."

"Huh?" David stood still, disconcerted. Sylvain looked up at him with eyes full of pain, his jaw tense, his lips a thin line. David slowly sat back down again.

CHAPTER 4

"My best friend's name was Stéphane. Stéphane Legendre. We'd been friends since we were kids. We practically grew up together, like brothers. Stéphane graduated from medical school near the top of his class and became a family doctor. He was very self-confident, verging on arrogant, good-looking, the kind of guy who has no doubts in life and is convinced of his own charm. He was kind of a dick, if I'm honest . . . but he was my friend.

"Late one afternoon, he called me in a complete panic. Three days before, he had written one of his patients a prescription unsuitable for pregnant women. He'd forgotten to ask her if she was pregnant, and of course she was. About three months along. She trusted him implicitly. The doctor gave her the prescription, so it must be fine, right? But then two days later, the day before he called me, she had a miscarriage. Her ob-gyn immediately made the connection and called Stéphane. In a panic, he denied prescribing the dose she'd taken and said what he'd prescribed was perfectly safe. They got into an argument. There were legal threats. He was facing a court case, damages, the whole thing. He'd just got off the phone that second. I could tell he was losing it, picturing himself in court, professional misconduct, guilty, punitive damages, banned from medical practice, maybe even prison . . ."

Sylvain fell silent for a brief moment, biting his lower lip, then picked the story up again.

"He told me the only proof was the prescription in his handwriting. So I, like a complete moron, said, 'So no prescription, no proof?' And he said yes. Simple. All it would take was switching the original prescription for one with the appropriate dose. All it would take . . . Easier said than done! What about the patient's copy? Stéphane said he could take care of that. We had the patient's address, so we checked her local drugstores. There were two. I went to the first one, right by her house. I had no real plan, and time was limited. If the prescription was the only proof Stéphane was in the wrong, it was bound to be crucial evidence in court. It might have even been too late. I decided to figure it out as I went along. I waited my turn in line, checking out the premises and watching the woman behind the counter. She took a prescription from the man in front of me, filled it, and put the paper in a drawer. Then it was my turn. I lied about a sore throat, asked for her opinion. She told me to go see a doctor. I laughed and told her I didn't trust them. 'They're all quacks, you go see them for a sore throat, you come out with prostate cancer!' She laughed too. I thought she was pretty when she laughed. She sold me some throat spray, I paid, and that was it. I left."

Sylvain sighed, shrugged, and continued his story.

"It was nearly closing time. Last chance. I went back in, said my throat was much better, thanks, would she care to join me for a quick drink in the bar next door? She laughed again, and hesitated. I said, just one drink. She told me to call a friend. I chuckled and said I didn't trust them: 'They're all after one thing, you buy them a drink and next thing you know, they want dinner too.' She laughed a third time, and I thought to myself, 'She is *really* pretty when she laughs.'"

Silence. Regret. Or perhaps remorse. David urged him on: "So, did you get the prescription?"

Sylvain nodded. "While she was getting changed and packing her stuff up in the back. She said, 'I'll just be a minute.' It was all so quick. I didn't stop to think, I hopped over the counter and searched the drawer. I remember counting the seconds, allowing myself up to sixty. At sixty, I would stop. Too risky. And I wasn't even sure it was the right drugstore. But luck was on my side. I found it very quickly. They were in chronological order, and I recognized Stéphane's writing immediately. I whipped it out and quickly slipped the replacement prescription in instead. I even had the presence of mind to ink it with the drugstore stamp by the cash register. Meanwhile, Stéphane went to talk to the patient to try to understand what had happened . . . and to switch over her copy. The poor woman fell for his performance, hook, line, and sinker. When he left, all proof of his mistake was gone."

"What happened then?"

Sylvain paused again. It was clear something was weighing on his conscience. That the words he had to say, even five years later, were as corrosive as acid.

"The pharmacist was sued for professional misconduct. She lost. The fake prescription 'proved' Stéphane's innocence, but the dose no longer matched what she had sold the patient. The problem was, I was still seeing her. I really liked her. I was falling in love like I never had before. It was a hellish situation. When it all started I never thought about what impact it might have on her, and when I realized she was in a world of shit and it was all my fault, I tried to pressure Stéphane into coming clean. The bastard refused. I threatened to go to the cops, even if it got me in trouble, and I swear I didn't care if it did. I was ready to make amends. But I knew I would lose her. I couldn't bear it. She is the love of my life. And the more time passed, the harder it was to confess."

Choked with emotions that were magnified and intensified by alcohol, Sylvain fell silent.

"What happened next?" David asked softly, putting his hand on his friend's shoulder.

Several seconds went by before Sylvain spoke again. "Like I said, she was found guilty of professional misconduct. She had to pay damages and she lost her license. In fact, she lost everything."

"And what did you do?"

"I stayed with her and helped her through it. To start with, I lent her the money she needed, and I wouldn't let her pay me back. We moved in together, and she retrained in horticulture. Time passed, she dug herself out of the hole, we moved to a new town, and here we are. The worst of it, I think, is her boundless gratitude. Sometimes she tells me that the whole trial thing was hard, of course, with the guilt—she just couldn't understand where she'd gone wrong—but she loves her life now so much more, and . . ."

Sylvain stopped again, trying to choke back the sobs rising

in his throat. "One thing's for sure—I owe her big time," he said. "A debt I'll never repay. She can ask me for anything. And I mean *anything*."

David smiled sadly. "What happened to your friend Stéphane in the end?"

Sylvain shook his head. "Never spoke to him again. We hold each other's fate in our hands. He can ruin my life, I can ruin his. We are poison to each other now."

"And Tiphaine still has no idea?"

"We're still together, aren't we? No, she has no clue."

"And you really think she'd leave you if she knew?"

Sylvain gave David a tortured look. "I *know* she would. She would stop me from ever seeing my son again and spend the rest of her life trying to destroy mine."

David pulled a wry face to suggest Sylvain was overexaggerating. Sylvain shot back, "What would you do in her shoes?"

David thought for a moment, and came to the same conclusion—of course she would leave. Rather than cheering Sylvain up, David's tacit agreement plunged him further into despair. Neither man spoke for a while.

Sylvain's tale had sobered David up. Sylvain, on the other hand, seemed drunker than ever. David decided enough was enough: time to stop sharing shattering secrets and bring the evening to an end. He stepped around the table, grabbed Sylvain by the waist, put his arm around his shoulders, hoisted him up, and steered him to the car.

As they were both buckling their seat belts for the ride home, David broke the silence, a note of bitterness in his voice. "Why did you tell me all that?"

Sylvain shrugged, as if it was all in the past. "Maybe so there's a chance she'll hear it from someone else one day . . . I've already tried telling her, but I just can't."

Irritation flashed across David's face. He turned the key in the ignition and turned to Sylvain. "Sorry, man, don't count on me to get involved in your private business. If you want her to know, you'll have to tell her yourself."

The morning after the strange evening when great joy had stood alongside tragedy, Sylvain called out to David from the doorstep as he left for work. "Have you got time for a quick coffee?"

David hesitated, glancing at his watch. Sylvain clearly had something on his mind. He followed Sylvain inside.

When they were sitting at the table, coffee in hand, Sylvain blurted out, "I . . . I wanted to say sorry for last night. I was drunk. I wasn't thinking straight, I didn't want to put you in an awkward situation . . ."

"Forget it," David reassured him with an understanding smile. "We'd both been drinking. Way too much. People get stupid when they're drunk."

"Not just when they're drunk," Sylvain mumbled.

David smiled in agreement.

"You know what I said in the car . . . ," Sylvain continued, his voice louder now. "Please, forget I ever said it."

"What are you talking about?"

"Promise me you'll never tell her! It *cannot* go any further. I don't know why I told you, I mean, I guess Maxime's arrival brought it all back and the booze made me overshare . . . I haven't slept a wink all night and . . ."

"Like I said," David interrupted him, "I have absolutely no intention of getting involved. We're friends, right?"

Sylvain gave a short, bitter laugh. "That's the problem. Last time I had a friend, look how it ended . . ."

"Listen, Sylvain. I mean, I wish you hadn't told me. But it's too late now. Let's just forget about it, right? Never mention it again."

Sylvain nodded.

"What about Laetitia?" he asked.

"What about her?"

"You haven't . . ."

"Of course not!"

"Thanks."

CHILD MEDICAL RECORD

6–7 MONTHS

Age your child began passing toys between their hands:

4.5 months

Age your child tried to sit up with your help:

5 months

Does your child turn their head when they hear a noise behind them?

Yes

How does your child show that they are tired?

M. wriggles a lot and cries about small things.

M. first went to daycare around 6 months old.
Slight cold, a few minor coughing fits, infrequent.

DOCTOR'S NOTES:

Weight: 21 lbs. 2 oz. Height: 2 ft. 5 in.
Oral thrush: apply miconazole four times daily after meals.
Nonallergic rhinitis: elevate the child's head overnight, flush his nose with saline solution, one squirt of Nesivine Baby nasal spray in each nostril three times daily for up to five days.

CHAPTER 5

Over the following months, the babies were all the couples talked about.

The two new mothers shared their worries, fears, and joys:

"His bottom is all red and raw and he cried all night. Do you think we should see a doctor?"

"Is he showing a temperature?"

"Ninety-nine point seven."

"Sounds like teething to me."

Meanwhile, the new fathers supported each other through the terrible ordeal of suddenly feeling less important and coping without sex:

"Feel like going to Simon's for a game of pool?"

"Definitely! I'll pick you up at eight, OK?"

"Great!"

They hung out at one house to feed the babies, then went next door for a drink, a change of scenery, to swap stories about sleepless nights. They lent each other diapers and baby Tylenol, and watched each other's babies while the parents went out for groceries or sometimes even stayed in for the supreme treat of an afternoon nap. Life followed an incessant rhythm of tiny daily miracles, accompanied by the unspoken yearning for freedoms now lost.

On Milo's first birthday, David and Laetitia had a special request for their friends.

"We'd like to have Milo baptized . . ."

"I didn't know you guys are Catholics!" Sylvain was surprised.

"I am, David isn't," Laetitia replied.

Sylvain turned to David in confusion. He just rolled his eyes and shrugged.

"Well, neither of us has any other family," Laetitia explained. "I haven't been to church in forever, and it's true I haven't been much of a believer these past few years. But . . ." She paused with a sigh. "I don't want to be a nuisance or impose my faith on anyone," she continued, a touch of embarrassment in her voice. "But I know my parents would have liked to see my son baptized, and even if they're not around anymore, I want to go ahead for their sakes. David and I have been talking a lot, and . . ."

"No worries," Tiphaine interrupted. "You don't need to explain. If you want to get Milo baptized, just do it, no problem!"

Laetitia cast her a grateful look.

"I . . . have you been baptized?"

"No, why?"

Tiphaine's response seemed to disappoint Laetitia. "Would you, if I asked you?"

"No way!" Tiphaine cried. "I'm a complete atheist! Why on earth would I?"

David intervened. "It's too much to ask, Laetitia. Forget it."

An embarrassed silence settled over the group. After a short while, Sylvain asked, "What's going on? What's the problem?"

"I think I know . . . ," Tiphaine murmured, staring at her friend. Laetitia was gazing at her with such hope in her eyes it took her breath away.

"Can someone fill me in?" Sylvain asked. "I have no idea what is going on."

Tiphaine sighed. "OK, fine," she said, her eyes locked on her friend's.

Laetitia's face lit up, she gave a squeal of delight and pulled Tiphaine in for a hug. Sylvain turned to David. "Do you have a clue what's going on? If you do, care to enlighten me?"

"Your wife has just agreed to be Milo's godmother," David said apologetically. "The problem is, she has to get herself baptized first."

CHAPTER 6

Not until the next day did Tiphaine realize what she had gotten herself into.

"A year and a half! Are you joking?"

"I know . . . ," Laetitia said pleadingly. "It sounds like a long time, but it won't take up much time day to day . . ."

"Laetitia! I love you and God knows I'd love to be Milo's godmother—there I go with the God stuff again—but don't ask me to go to special God classes and all that nonsense! A year and a half of religious instruction, just to get sprinkled with a few drops of water . . ."

"Not just a few drops!" Laetitia exclaimed with disarming honesty. "It's full immersion for adults."

"You're joking! No way I'm doing that. It's all nonsense as far as I'm concerned anyway."

Laetitia paused, gathering her thoughts, then spoke with a sigh. "I thought this might happen. When you said yes, I went home and looked up the process for adults. I saw what a big ask it was, taking special classes, following the various liturgical stages of joining the church, all the steps it would take . . . and I was sure you'd change your mind. So I researched a bit more. Turns out you don't have to be baptized,

29

as long as the godfather is. You would be a kind of unofficial godmother, and to keep things fair, we'll hold a civil naming ceremony too."

"What does that change?"

"Nothing, from our point of view."

"What's the catch, then?"

"No catch."

Tiphaine gave a satisfied nod. Then, realizing what Laetitia had said, she asked, "So who's the godfather then?"

"Ernest."

When Tiphaine thought about it, it made sense. She was surprised she hadn't thought of him herself. Ernest was the probation officer assigned to help David get back on his feet after his release from prison. He was now sixty-five, blunt and outspoken, his face etched with the lines of a hard life. He smoked like a chimney and swore like a sailor, and his views were as rigid as his posture. Early in his career he had been held hostage by a "client" and ended up with a bullet through his shin at close range, leaving him with a pronounced limp and an unbending attitude toward the former prisoners he worked with. His intransigence had been exactly what David needed to stop him from getting back into drugs and crime.

David owed him everything.

Over the years, their working relationship had softened into a friendship rooted in trust and mutual respect. Ernest was now the closest thing David had to a father. He had no wife or children of his own. He lived alone in a one-room apartment on the east side of Paris and treasured his independence fiercely.

Tiphaine was intrigued. "So Ernest is baptized, then?"

Laetitia nodded. Tiphaine pursed her lips in surprise. "I'd never have guessed."

The church baptism was held three months later. It was a modest ceremony, with just five people present: the happy parents, Tiphaine and Sylvain, and Ernest. He had dressed up for the occasion for once, squeezing into a three-piece suit he clearly hadn't worn for several years. His posture in the too-tight suit heightened a certain awkwardness that the circumstances did little to alleviate. He was clearly tense, embarrassed, and feeling out of place. But when David had asked him to be Milo's godfather, Ernest's heart, hardened by years on his own, melted.

"You know, kids aren't really my thing" was his initial reaction when David got in touch. "Diapers, bottles, coochie coochie coo, all that stuff is a mystery to me."

"Well, now's your chance to learn!"

Ernest nodded vaguely and asked for a few days to think about it. David and Laetitia didn't hear from him for two weeks. Then one late Wednesday afternoon he showed up at their house with a bottle of wine in one hand, a teddy bear in the other.

"I'll do it!" he declared, as if accepting a dangerous mission. "But I'm warning you now, don't count on me to take him to the playground, babysit, or read him sappy stories. I'm not about to start all that at my age."

But being the boy's godfather softened his attitude little by little. He came to visit more often and took more and more interest in Milo—almost reluctantly, it seemed. When, one day,

Milo wordlessly held out his favorite book, Ernest took it, settled the boy on his knees, and read the sappy story to him in his gravelly voice, unable to mask the joy he felt in sharing such a simple pleasure with his godson.

The priest's voice echoed around the church. The twenty rows of chairs were unoccupied except for Tiphaine and Sylvain at the front. David and Laetitia stood at the altar with Ernest, who was holding Milo.

"Now I turn to you, the child's parents and godfather. Through the sacrament of baptism, the child will be granted a new life by God's love. He will be born anew of water and the Holy Spirit. His life in God will encounter many obstacles. He will need your guidance to defeat sin and grow in faith. If you are guided by faith and are willing to guide him in turn, I ask you today, reminding you of your own baptism, to renounce sin and to proclaim your faith in Jesus Christ."

David, Laetitia, and Ernest followed the priest in rejecting sin, evil, and Satan and reaffirming their faith in God, Christ, the Holy Spirit, the forgiveness of sins, the resurrection of the flesh, and eternal life. Then the priest sprinkled holy water on Milo, who squawked in displeasure at the splash of cold water in the unheated church.

The civil naming ceremony the following week at the town hall was much less formal. The mayor had been busy celebrating weddings all morning and was eager for his lunch. Like Ernest the week before, Tiphaine had dressed for the occasion. Unlike Ernest, she looked wonderful. Sylvain was looking after Maxime in his stroller. Ernest also came. The registrar attended to the paperwork while the mayor read out the undertakings Tiphaine promised to honor: to protect the child, to ensure he received an education free from social, philosophical, and religious prejudice, to bring him up to respect the institutions of democracy, to model the moral, human, and civic qualities required of a citizen devoted to the public good and to liberty, and to foster understanding, brotherhood, and solidarity toward his fellow men. Tiphaine agreed with a sense of solemnity that even surprised herself. Inwardly she had thought that the ceremony was completely pointless: she felt like she had become Milo's second mother the second he was born and no official paperwork could change or add to that in any way. Yet as she listened to the mayor, the seriousness of the undertaking moved her more than she had anticipated. Her hand trembled slightly as she signed the document.

Maxime, now three and a half, asks for some grenadine syrup and water. Tiphaine reminds him: "What's the magic word?"

"Please."

Pouring the syrup into his glass, Tiphaine explains, "See, now I can serve you grenadine with pleasure."

"And with water!" Maxime clarifies.

CHAPTER 7

Sundays are for families. Some sit through a long lunch with extended family, forcing themselves to go through with the ritual every week even though they dream of canceling. For the grandparents. And because that's the way it's always been—the grandparents would never see the kids otherwise. Every week, the parents wonder why they bother as the clock strikes four, giving them an excuse to leave: there's school tomorrow, it'll be late by the time we get home and the kids still have to finish their homework . . .

Why *do* we keep on visiting? Why every Sunday? We have nothing left to talk about, we don't agree on anything, we made different choices in life. So why do we force ourselves through it?

The nagging question comes up relentlessly on the drive home, along with barbed comments about your sister-in-law's outfit, your teenage nephew's worrisome views—he's heading for trouble, that boy—and your mother's deafness, it's getting worse, and I mean yes, I know too much salt is bad for you but I think my arteries could cope with a *little* flavor!

You sigh, you grumble, you often end up arguing. Driving home from Sunday lunch with the parents—or worse, the in-laws—is prime time for snapping at each other, sulking until dinner, and swearing that this was the absolute last time, next week you're on your own!

And the next week, you're back again. Because that's the way it is.

Other people—ones without extended families, or at least without families within easy driving range—stay at home and look after their own kids. Play with trains. Paint. Mess around with Play-Doh, if they feel like it. Watch a cartoon, always the same one, reeling off the dialogue and singing along to the soundtrack. It brings a smile to their faces at first, but after a while they've had enough. SpongeBob's voice is seriously annoying.

It's almost as if Sundays were invented to make couples argue. Ones with children, anyway. Before kids come along, Sundays are for lazing around in bed, waking up at noon, breakfast at one, then back to bed for a bit of adult playtime. Then whatever they feel like, depending on the weather. A nice walk, a drink at a sidewalk terrace in the sun, a movie on rainy days.

But that was before. Once the kids come along, those days are gone.

That might explain why every Sunday at around five, Tiphaine and Sylvain would come knocking on David and Laetitia's door, their barely finished quarrel etched on their faces. The Brunelles always welcomed them with open arms: a whole day of looking after a kid, building wooden block castles, and playing Hungry Hungry Hippos is enough to get on anyone's nerves, especially when one parent is a more active participant than the other. They would all hang out together, rounding off a long day full of active passivity spent glancing at watches that seemed to be at a standstill by enjoying an aperitif or a late-afternoon snack.

On one such Sunday, it was sunny, and they were planning to relax on the Brunelles' terrace.

"We're having a little birthday party for Milo next week," Laetitia said, reaching into the cupboard for the glasses. "Are you guys free?"

"Next week!" Tiphaine exclaimed. "Four already! It's gone by so quick. Do we have anything planned, Sylvain?"

"Not that I know of," he mumbled, barely glancing in her direction as he headed for the terrace.

"Another fight in the car, huh?" Laetitia inquired discreetly, searching the kitchen drawers.

Tiphaine rolled her eyes and sighed. "Jesus. Next week I am staying home, that's for sure!"

"You say that every week!" giggled Laetitia. Then she called out to the terrace, "David, have you seen the corkscrew?"

"In the drawer. Where it always is."

"If it was in the drawer I wouldn't be asking, would I?" she snapped.

"You guys sound pretty on edge too," whispered Tiphaine.

"Ugh, don't ask." Laetitia sighed, her irritation clear. She called out to the terrace again, "David, if you want some red wine you're going to have to get it yourself, I can't find the corkscrew anywhere!"

David stomped into the kitchen and started looking. The corkscrew was nowhere to be found.

"Want to bet Milo has been playing with it again?"

"Don't worry about it," Tiphaine chimed in. She poked her head through the kitchen window and called to Sylvain, "Can you go and get our corkscrew?"

"Why don't you go?"

"Sylvain!"

He got up reluctantly, dug for his keys in his pocket, and headed for the front door. The two women rolled their eyes behind his back, smiled conspiratorially at each other, and took the drinks and snacks out. When Sylvain was back, David uncorked the wine and poured himself and Tiphaine a glass. Laetitia had a pastis and Sylvain some port. They all clinked glasses and began to chat, forgetting their annoyances.

"Where are the boys?" Laetitia suddenly asked worriedly, realizing they hadn't seen them for a while.

"At the far end of the yard," Sylvain said, pointing.

Squinting in the low sun, Tiphaine spotted the children busy tunneling through the hedge separating the two yards.

"What are they up to?"

"Making a secret passage," David said. "Milo told me yesterday they wanted to open up a hole in the hedge to get between the yards more easily."

"My hedge!" lamented Laetitia.

"What do you mean, your hedge? It's ours as much as yours," teased Tiphaine.

The four of them wandered down to the lawn, glasses in hand, to see what the boys were up to. They all had something to say:

"It might not be the best place for a hole in the hedge . . ."

"Of course it is! If they really want to ruin the hedge, best place for it is down here where it's not too visible."

"The rate they're going, they won't have finished by Christmas!"

"Yes, we will!" exclaimed Maxime. "We can already squeeze through." He demonstrated, wriggling between the branches he and Milo had already pulled aside, forcing his way through a gap that was clearly still too narrow for him.

"Stop it, Maxime!" Tiphaine shouted. "You're going to ruin Laetitia's hedge!"

"It's your hedge as much as it is mine," Laetitia laughed, imitating Tiphaine.

"Yes, but this is your side of it!"

"Not a bad idea, though, is it?" mused Sylvain.

"What?"

"Opening up the hedge between our yards."

Sylvain's suggestion was met with thoughtful silence, so he continued. "We could open up a proper passageway. I mean, we're constantly in each other's yard anyway, and it would be more practical when we can't find things like the corkscrew, so that we don't have to go around through the front door . . ."

They all stared at the hedge, imagining what it would be like to have direct access to the neighbors' yard. Laetitia pictured a low white gate that pushed open. Tiphaine imagined a proper gate with a low wall she could train climbing plants over, maybe even topped with little red tiles. Sylvain pictured a wrought-iron fence. David pictured nothing: he was not sure he liked the idea.

"The problem is I'm not sure Mrs. Coustenoble would agree," Tiphaine pointed out, to David's relief: he would not have to be the bad guy after all.

Mrs. Coustenoble was Tiphaine and Sylvain's landlady—a widow who did not seem to miss her late husband, Gilbert, much at all. She was the very model of the type of landlady who seemed kind but whose tolerance and understanding were pushed to their limits whenever anything came up at the house that she needed to deal with. She was a withered-looking woman of about sixty, generally discreet but mistrustful when it came to touching her house and gardening in any way, even to making improvements. Sylvain, an architect by profession, had already suggested changing the layout of some rooms, sharing the cost and adding value to the house while making it more livable for the family. She had always said no. Mrs. Coustenoble's name was like an evil shadow hanging over the Geniot family's dreams of interior design, of making their home truly their own—unlike the Brunelles, who luckily owned their house.

The difference in home-ownership status between the two couples was a standing joke, a cause for friendly teasing. Tiphaine and Sylvain were much better off than David, a taxi driver, and Laetitia, a social worker, who sometimes struggled at the end of the month. Tiphaine and Sylvain were not wealthy by any means, but they were significantly more comfortable—though they were still renters, which evened out the balance. They did not discuss money much. The Geniots took longer, sunnier holidays than the Brunelles, but their dreams of splashing out on home decor were usually dashed by Mrs. Coustenoble's reluctance.

"We could at least ask her," Sylvain said.

"Forget it!" Tiphaine sighed. "You can be sure that old cow will say no before we've even got the words out."

"Well, let's see . . . if she says no, it's too bad, but at least we will have tried!"

Leaving the children to their own devices, they headed back to the terrace, chatting about what kind of gate they would like, how much it might cost, and the best place to put it in. David secretly prayed that Tiphaine's fears were well founded.

CHAPTER 8

Laetitia carried in a magnificent chocolate cake with four candles, singing "Happy Birthday." All the guests quickly joined in. She put the cake down in front of Milo, whose face was flushed red with pride and delight. He took a deep breath and noisily puffed out the candles, to thunderous applause.

They had invited six of Milo's school friends as well as Maxime, Tiphaine, and Sylvain. Some had come with their mothers, others with both parents and their big brothers and baby sisters. The party was in full swing, and the Brunelle house was bursting at the seams. David and Laetitia were running around cutting slices of cake, pouring drinks, careful you don't spill it, spoons are in the second drawer down in the kitchen, setting up party games, chatting with the other parents, so you're a journalist, that's interesting, can I get you another coffee?

Ernest stopped by briefly to wish his godson a happy birthday. He brought an impressive pair of boxing gloves that had once belonged to a long-forgotten professional boxer, making Milo the envy of his classmates and earning a disapproving sniff from Laetitia.

"Ernest, what were you thinking? You can't give a four-year-old boxing gloves!"

"Really? Why not?"

She was just about to reply when one of the children burst out into loud sobs. Milo had put one of the gloves on and tried it out on his friend.

"That's why!" she cried over her shoulder, rushing over to the sobbing boy. She gave him a hug and confiscated the gloves. Milo protested, Laetitia raised her voice, some of the children tried to grab the gloves. Mutiny was in the air.

"Who wants to play musical chairs?" David called out, loud enough for everyone to hear. The rebels dropped the idea of rioting and rushed headlong into David's trap. Ten seconds later, calm was restored. Laetitia offered Ernest coffee.

After the party, as the last few guests were leaving, Laetitia, David, Tiphaine, and Sylvain slumped onto the living room sofa and chairs, squashing a few cake crumbs and stray pieces of candy.

"The next party will be when he turns twenty, and he can plan it himself!" Laetitia groaned, surveying the indescribable mess in the room.

"Wait until you see his bedroom!" David murmured, rubbing his neck.

"Would you like to send Milo over to our house for a sleepover?" offered Tiphaine. "That way you can clean up without him getting in your way."

"Feel free to keep him all week! I've had enough of kids for a while!"

They all laughed and began gossiping about the party. "Wow, doesn't that Grégoire boy look like his father? The kid's practically a clone!"

"Firmin's mother is not the most approachable, is she?"

"Which was one was Firmin? Ah yeah, the little blond kid with a squint."

Suddenly Sylvain sat up straight in his armchair. "Hey guys, guess what, we forgot the good news! Mrs. Coustenoble is on board for the hedge idea!"

Laetitia was feeling drained, but she mustered enough energy to show some enthusiasm. They began discussing the gate. Laetitia mentioned her idea for a low white country gate. The simpler, the better. Wrought iron? Yes, that would be pretty. But more expensive, surely?

"Don't worry about the cost of the labor, we'll pay," Sylvain reassured her.

"What sort of cost are we talking?"

"Not much, we're looking at around a thousand euros."

"A thousand!" Laetitia exclaimed. "We can't afford that!"

"But you'd only be paying half," Tiphaine pointed out.

"Even so . . ."

"What do you think, David?" Sylvain asked.

David looked embarrassed, sighed, and took the plunge.

"I'm not sure it's a good idea," he said in a serious tone, at odds with the cheery conversation.

"What's not a good idea?"

"Opening up a gate in the hedge."

"Why not?"

"The reason we are such good friends is *because* we don't

44

live together. We each have our own space, we're not constantly in each other's faces. When we ring your bell, if you don't feel like opening the door, you don't have to. Same for us. And it works."

"We've never pretended to be out when you rang," Sylvain replied slowly, taken aback.

"Nor have we!" Laetitia chimed in apologetically.

"Well then . . ."

"OK, that was a bad example." David sighed. "You know what I mean."

His reluctance cast a pall over the room. Laetitia, Tiphaine, and Sylvain gazed at him in surprise and confusion for a few seconds.

"Why are you only saying this now?" Laetitia said, astonished at her husband's reaction.

"I can't see why a gate between the two yards should change anything," objected a disappointed Tiphaine.

"In theory, it probably wouldn't. But in practice . . . we'd be tempted to cut through because it'd be quicker and easier."

It was clear to the other three that there was little point in discussing the cost and style of gate. Silence filled the room, indicating their disappointment. Eventually Sylvain cracked a joke to lighten the atmosphere.

"OK, I get it, you and Laetitia like to get freaky on the living room sofa and we'd be able to see you from the garden . . ."

"That's part of it," David said, his face perfectly straight.

"It's a great reason," Sylvain replied with a wink to Laetitia.

Tiphaine, slumped on the sofa, sprang up to fetch herself coffee.

"OK," she conceded with a tone of regret. "You could have said, though, before we wasted our time asking Mrs. Coustenoble." She grabbed a chair and pulled it over to sit down.

David nodded. "I'm sorry. You seemed so sure she would nix the idea, I didn't want to pour cold water on it."

They stared at each other for a moment. It was clear from Tiphaine's expression that she was toying with the idea of trying to change David's mind. Then she gave a rueful smile and shrugged. "Ah well, never mind!"

CHILD MEDICAL RECORD

AGE 4 TO 5

Can your child dress themself?

Yes, with some help.

Is your child's speech clear to people they don't know?

M. is a chatterbox, his speech is great!

Does your child take part in class?

It depends on his mood. I don't think he enjoys music and movement classes much. But he loves construction sets, drawing, and singing.

DOCTOR'S NOTES:

Weight: 40 lbs. 6 oz. Height: 3 ft. 6 in.
Throat infection, temperature 102.2°. Antibiotics: 5 ml of Augmentin 3 times a day at mealtimes for a week.
5 ml of Junifen for fevers over 100.5°. Left ear blocked.

CHAPTER 9

That year, fall was heralded by days of gray skies. By early October, both families had put away their outdoor furniture, folded up the deck chairs, and put the protective cover over the table. Rain had stopped all talk of opening up the hedge. They still rang at each other's front door for now.

Early one Tuesday afternoon, David was reading the newspaper in his taxi outside the station, hoping for a few customers from the 2:09 train from Paris. Finishing the sports page, he folded the paper and tucked it away in the glove compartment. He glanced at his watch then turned his gaze to the main entrance of the station. A handful of passengers were trickling out. A mother and her daughter headed straight for the bus stop. Two young men rushed into the car in front of his taxi. A woman around fifty years old paced the sidewalk slowly, lighting a cigarette. She pulled hard on it and blew out the smoke with an expression of deep contentment, glancing left and right as she waited. David decided to wait until she finished her cigarette before asking if she wanted a ride, if no one else showed up in the meantime.

He never knew if anyone came to pick her up: a few seconds later, a man slid into his back seat. "Rue Edmond-Petit," he said.

David nodded, switched on his meter, and drove off. The address was more than familiar. It was his own street. He said nothing, not feeling like making polite conversation.

David was not a chatty taxi driver. He was irritated by idle chatter whose only purpose was to break an awkward silence. He was not interested in bonding with perfect strangers he would never see again once they got out of his taxi. And most of all, no one was paying him to talk.

What he did like was scrutinizing the people in the back seat. Keeping his eyes on the road, he just had to shift his gaze an inch or two to the right to watch their expressions in his rearview mirror. He'd notice how they watched the world go by, curious or contemplative, and how they talked on their cell phones, discussing their work or their private lives with no holds barred as if he simply didn't exist. He had always been amazed at how many people seemed to believe that taxi drivers had no ears, no opinions, as if he were just a pair of eyes following the road, hands gripping the steering wheel, feet on the gas pedal and brake.

David had a flair for watching his customers undetected. As he stared at their reflections, he had a sixth sense for when they would feel him studying them and lift their eyes to the little rearview mirror. By the time they focused on it David already had his eyes fixed on the road ahead. The most suspicious passengers checked several times, but he always outsmarted them. He could spot the exact microsecond when they blinked before looking up at the mirror, only to find him looking ahead at the road, his expression neutral.

He enjoyed studying his customers. This one was no different. He was roughly the same age as David, around thirty-five, and dressed sharply in a well-cut, elegant suit. A well-heeled man confident of his own opinions. He was quite good-looking, though his face was wan, etched with deep exhaustion, his eyes ringed, his cheeks sunken. His gaze was unsettled, flicking from side to side, studying the streets, looking for landmarks, memorizing the route. Nervous. In a hurry. What else? Nothing.

Having gleaned all he could from a surreptitious study, David turned his focus back to the road.

"Here we are," he said, turning right into Rue Edmond-Petit.

"Number twenty-six, please," added the man.

David chuckled inwardly. Tiphaine and Sylvain's house. He took a longer look at the man, wondering which of the two he was visiting. It must be Sylvain, who often had architect colleagues visiting from Paris.

He briefly toyed with the idea of telling the man he knew Sylvain Geniot, they were close friends, that he lived next door. Quite a coincidence, huh? But he said nothing. What would be the point?

David pulled up outside the front door. He stopped the meter and waited as the customer paid and stepped out of the car. For a second or two, he was tempted to stop at home for five minutes and coffee, but glanced at the dashboard clock and decided to wait until later.

As he drove off, he saw the man ringing Tiphaine and Sylvain's front doorbell.

CHAPTER 10

David did not mention dropping the man off at his house to Sylvain. At least, not straight away. It was not that he wanted to keep it a secret, or even that he forgot about it. He simply never got the opportunity to chat about such a mundane event. He didn't see Sylvain until the following Friday, for drinks.

The day before, anxiety had begun to gnaw at him as he read the paper in his taxi.

He had been back at the station again, waiting for customers. As he turned to the sports pages, his eye was caught by a photograph. He looked closely, surprised to recognize the customer he had dropped off at the Geniots' house the previous Tuesday. The caption shocked him. The man was a family doctor from Paris named Stéphane Legendre. Suffering from terminal pancreatic cancer, he had been found dead in his office the previous Wednesday morning, a syringe half-full of cyanide dangling from one arm. The police quickly decided it could not have been murder. There was no sign of forced entry or violence. Nothing was missing. No suspicious fingerprints. They ruled it was suicide, triggered by the terminal cancer diagnosis. Clearly, the doctor had decided not to prolong the agony of a slow, painful death.

The article included a brief statement by his secretary. Dr. Legendre had not shared his diagnosis with her, but he had seemed rather low in mood of late. Since their relationship was purely professional, she had never imagined he was depressed enough to take his own life. If only she'd known!

Stéphane Legendre. A family doctor in Paris. David suddenly recalled Sylvain's story about how he and Tiphaine first met: the ex–best friend too arrogant to make amends for his own mistakes. The doctor with the tragic miscarriage on his conscience. The doctor who had seen Tiphaine face the court for his own professional misconduct. No doubt about it—it was the same man.

David put down the newspaper thoughtfully, Sylvain's words echoing through his mind. *"We hold each other's fate in our hands. He can ruin my life, I can ruin his. We are poison to each other now."* Furrowing his brow, he thought back to the man's attitude in the back seat of his taxi two days before. He had studied him carefully in the rearview mirror. The man had seemed haggard, somber, withdrawn. The signs David had read as deep exhaustion were the marks of the disease eating away at him.

"Avenue Victor Hugo, please," said a young woman as she slid onto the back seat. The slam of the car door stirred David from his thoughts. He nodded, started the meter, and drove off.

The next day, the four friends met for happy hour, as they did every Friday. The end of the working week meant kicking back a little. Maxime and Milo were generously allowed to stay up later to watch TV, mainly so the adults could enjoy a drink without being disturbed. It suited everyone and they all enjoyed the change of pace.

A whole day had gone by since David read the paper. The first shock had faded. David had initially planned not to say anything—after all, it was none of his business really—but curiosity got the better of him. While Laetitia and Tiphaine were chatting in the kitchen, he pulled Sylvain aside.

"I know I promised never to talk about it," he murmured, "but it was me who picked your doctor friend up from the station on Tuesday and brought him to your place."

"What are you talking about?" Sylvain stared at David in confusion.

He really did not seem to have a clue what David meant. David immediately explained.

"Your old friend Stéphane Legendre, the one who . . ." Sylvain turned pale when he heard the name. He gestured frantically to David to stop talking, glancing anxiously toward the kitchen.

"It's fine, she can't hear us," whispered David.

Sylvain checked the women were still out of earshot, then turned back to his friend. "What about Stéphane Legendre?" he asked nervously.

"I dropped him off at your house on Tuesday."

"Jesus Christ, David!" Sylvain flared. "What are you trying to tell me?"

"Nothing!" David shot back, offended. "I mean, I'm not going to pretend I didn't see it! He got in my taxi on Tuesday and I dropped him at your house, and by Wednesday morning he was dead in his office."

"*What?*"

Sylvain's face went from pale to livid. He leaned heavily on the nearby table and gazed at David in horror. "What are you telling me?" His voice was barely a whisper.

David was staggered: Sylvain clearly had no idea that his old friend had visited, or that he was suddenly, and horribly, dead. "You . . . you didn't ask him to come visit you, this past Tuesday, around half past two?"

"Tuesday? I . . ."

Sylvain seemed too shaken up to think. He gaped at David, his eyes aghast, his brain imploding from the relentless attack of a platoon of thoughts, each more explosive than the last.

David was lost for words, watching powerlessly as his friend seemed to struggle to free himself from the grip of anguish, his eyes flitting around the room.

Suddenly, Sylvain frowned. "I wasn't even at home on Tuesday afternoon!" he said, his voice flat.

He turned back to the kitchen, his eyes haunted, watching Tiphaine through the frosted glass of the kitchen door. A frank peal of laughter curled through the air.

David grasped Sylvain's worst fear, and simply asked, "What about Tiphaine?"

Sylvain shook his head. "Not that I know of," he added.

David shrugged. "Well then, there's only one explanation I can think of. Your old friend, knowing he was about to die, came to see you one last time. Maybe to beg for your forgiveness. Unburden his conscience and die with his soul at rest. Since no one was in, he went back to his office and took his own life."

"He killed himself?"

"Seems to be what the police think. Injected himself with cyanide."

Sylvain grimaced in horror.

"I'm sorry," David murmured. "I thought you knew."

"You look like you've seen a ghost, the pair of you!" Laetitia exclaimed, coming into the living room. "Sweetheart, Tiphaine is offering us some tomato and lettuce seedlings. We could dig a little patch for Milo at the end of the yard for him to grow his own organic vegetables. I always wanted to be the crunchy-mom type!"

David reacted fast to cover for Sylvain, giving him time to pull himself together. He walked over to his wife with a broad smile.

"What a great idea! Then we'll raise chickens and rabbits and declare our independence!"

Tiphaine came in. He asked her, "Tell me if I'm wrong, but this isn't exactly planting season, is it?"

She nodded. "For tomatoes, you'll have to wait until March. But we're getting rid of a lot of seeds and plants at work, and for lettuce you can start in January. You can just keep them in the shed."

"Great!" David declared enthusiastically.

"What were you two talking about?" asked Laetitia, her face quizzical.

"Nothing special, why?"

"I just didn't think you'd be so excited about a vegetable patch . . ."

"What's that got to do with anything?"

Laetitia gave him a loving smile. "Nothing." She kissed him, then turned to Sylvain. "Do you guys want to stay for dinner?"

Sylvain had managed to pull himself together. He agreed with slightly forced enthusiasm, which Tiphaine picked up on. "Would you rather go home?"

"Not at all!" he responded awkwardly.

Tiphaine gave him a suspicious look. "Everything OK?"

Knowing his acting skills would never fool her, he came up with a hasty excuse. "I think my blood pressure is a little low, I don't feel great . . ."

"Oh, sweetheart!" Tiphaine exclaimed, a worried note in her voice. "I'm always telling you you work too much. Sit down on the sofa, Laetitia and I will sort out dinner."

Laetitia turned to her husband. "David, can you tear the boys away from the TV? They've been glued to it for over an hour."

If the women were going to be in charge of cooking, no reason the men should take it easy—they could be in charge of the boys.

David nodded. When the women were back in the kitchen, he went over to sit with Sylvain on the sofa. "Are you going to be OK?"

Now Tiphaine was out of the way, Sylvain's distress was clear from his expression.

"That really doesn't sound like him!"

"What doesn't?"

Lost in thought, Sylvain said nothing for a while. Then he looked up and gazed at David, his eyes full of emotion. "Coming to beg for forgiveness, then taking his own life . . . he must have had another reason for wanting to see me."

"What sort of reason?"

"I have no idea. But nothing good, that's for sure."

AT THE SWIMMING POOL

Tiphaine and Laetitia are chatting away by the edge of the swimming pool while Maxime and Milo shriek and play in the kiddie pool. Milo, now almost five, gets out of the water and takes off his swimsuit.

Laetitia asks in surprise, "Milo, why have you taken off your swimsuit?"

"Because it's all wet, Mom!"

CHAPTER 11

"That's *enough*!" Laetitia yelled in exasperation, striding into Milo's bedroom. "You boys really need to keep the noise down! We can hear you downstairs in the kitchen . . ."

Her words trailed off into silence as she surveyed the wreckage. The toy shelves were completely empty, their contents strewn across the carpet. She couldn't even see what color it was anymore. It wouldn't have mattered so much if the games were all in their boxes, but Maxime and Milo had emptied them all and jumbled up the pieces to form a muddled, multicolored heap in which Laetitia spotted pieces of various jigsaws, Connect 4, picture bingos, all the Playmobil toys with their various accessories, Kapla blocks, dominoes, pickup sticks, the dismantled wooden racing track, felt-tipped pens and colored pencils, and the card games Milo loved so much, like Uno, Seven Families, and Top Trumps. The two boys froze, caught in the act when Laetitia burst in. Maxime's back was to the door but he was clearly sitting comfortably astride Milo on the bed. Permanent marker pen in hand, he was busy drawing a handsome mustache, 1970s-style glasses, a bushy beard, and what seemed to be an assortment of facial scars on his friend.

Laetitia took one look at the mess on her son's bedroom floor. She made for the bed and saw her son's new look. Maxime turned toward her: his own face was covered in colorful scribbles, far more than Milo's.

"Have you gone mad?"

The two boys burst out laughing.

"Don't we look great, Mom!" Milo exclaimed, sitting up to let her admire Maxime's handiwork.

"Milo! Maxime! What on earth are you doing?"

"We're playing at being old," Maxime said, a note of pride in his voice.

Laetitia realized the lines on Milo's face were not meant to be scars, but wrinkles. "Well, stop it now! Maxime, give me that pen right now!"

She stumbled on a toy as she stepped forward, nearly twisting her ankle. She picked her way through the heap, grabbed both boys, and dragged them to the bathroom to scrub at their faces. Most of the ink stayed put.

"Your mother is going to kill me . . . ," she muttered, looking despairingly at Maxime's little ink-covered face.

"Don't you like it?" asked Milo, looking at his mother with an expression of surprised disappointment.

"No, I do not!" cried Laetitia. "I don't like it when you misbehave, I don't like it when you make a mess everywhere, I don't like it when the pair of you act like little devils! Milo, what on earth were you thinking? Have you seen the state of your bedroom? Any more of this behavior and you'll both be in big trouble!"

"What sort of trouble?" Maxime wanted to know. Laetitia thought for a moment.

"Later, when you're all grown up, you'll have children as difficult as you are."

"How do you know?"

"Because when I was a little girl I misbehaved all the time. And my mom would always say one day I'd have a child as difficult as I was and then I would understand. And that would be my punishment. Well, here you go: I have a very bad little boy."

"That doesn't make any sense," argued Milo.

"Why not?"

"Because if I am good because I don't want a bad boy or girl when I grow up, it means you'll never be punished for all the bad things you did when you were little."

Laetitia gave her son a weary look, torn between a withering put-down and just ending the debate right there. She spent a few long seconds trying to think of an argument that would shut his smart mouth once and for all. Eventually she opted for silence, putting on a cartoon to keep them from making any more mess.

"So as a reward for making a huge mess and drawing on each other's face, you let them watch TV?" Tiphaine asked in astonishment when she came to pick up Maxime. "Well, that's an unusual approach to improving behavior."

"I was hardly going to whip them, was I?" Laetitia retorted. "They're only five . . . I mean, of course they're bound to act up from time to time . . ."

"And of course they should be punished for it," Tiphaine snapped. "Boys will be boys, but it's up to us to guide them."

Laetitia sighed. "Give me a break, Tiphaine. What are you trying to tell me? I'm bringing my son up all wrong?"

Tiphaine hesitated, then decided to speak up. "I think he needs stronger boundaries. I mean, think about it! Whenever you guys have Maxime, they get up to all sorts of trouble! And the only thing you ever do is stick them in front of the TV."

"I stuck them in front of the TV, as you put it, because I knew you'd be here in under half an hour!"

"And, well, I mean . . . it wouldn't even occur to me to leave them alone together in Maxime's room."

"What exactly do you think will happen to them?"

"That!" Tiphaine exclaimed, pointing at her son's face.

"Oh, come on . . . it's not like they were in any danger! Just give him a good bath tonight and it'll be fine."

Tiphaine heaved a deep sigh, flopped down onto a kitchen chair, and lit a cigarette. "Sorry. I'm a bit wound up these days."

"Anything going on?" Laetitia asked, sitting down alongside her.

"Nothing. Everything. Work. My mom. Sylvain."

"Well, get it off your chest. Start from the beginning."

"I don't feel like talking about it. Can I have coffee?"

Laetitia fetched two coffee cups from the cupboard and ran the espresso machine. She cracked open the window to air the kitchen. Tiphaine understood the message, glancing at her sidelong but not stubbing out her cigarette.

"You are wound up, aren't you!" Laetitia commented as she set the cups down on the table.

"I'm tired. I need a vacation."

"You guys going anywhere nice this year?"

Tiphaine rolled her eyes. "Sylvain's parents are insisting we visit them in Normandy."

"And?"

"It's not exactly the most exciting prospect!"

"It doesn't sound like Sylvain to want to spend his vacation with his parents, does it?"

"His dad isn't doing too well, so he said OK. He said it might be his last year . . ."

"If you're that reluctant, why don't you let him take Maxime to their place for a few days? Then you can head off somewhere nice, just the three of you, for a real break. That way, everybody's happy."

Tiphaine gave a bitter laugh. "Oh, I wish! You have no idea of the repercussions if I did that. It would be World War Three. They would never ever let me forget it! And Sylvain has declared that if I don't put up with his parents in Normandy this summer, he doesn't see why he should put up with mine next Christmas. We had Christmas with his parents last year, so my mom will freak out if we don't go to hers this year. So I'm stuck." Tiphaine shrugged, staring deep into her cup as if the answer to all her woes lay at the bottom. "The problem is, Sylvain doesn't get along with his family. Even when he was a kid, he was always fighting with his parents and his brother and sister. So when it comes down to it, family stuff is a huge pain in the ass for him. You cannot even imagine what it's like when they all get together. Constant shouting, blaming each other for this and that. No warmth, no sense of togetherness, no fun. Just stress, and I loathe it."

"Have you said anything to him?"

"That's not the problem."

"What is the problem, then?"

"Sylvain is just the same with my family, constantly nit-picking and unpleasant. It's like he can't even process that we might get on well and I enjoy spending time with them."

"I don't get it."

"Sylvain can't stand my mom and dad or my brother. Not because they don't get along . . . I mean, they don't, but only because they're my family. I bet if he met them in the normal course of events, he would think they were fine."

She paused, thinking about what she had just said, and corrected herself. "I mean, I don't think he would hate them as much."

Laetitia nodded to show she understood. Tiphaine continued, "I'm beginning to think he's just jealous of how well we all get on, my parents, my brother, and me. That somewhere deep down inside, he holds it against me. It's like his family makes him unhappy, so I can't be happy with mine. And I can't stand that! I'm always so pleased to see my parents, spend time with them, chat and have fun together . . . These days, when they invite us over, I'm always on the defensive because I know Sylvain is miserable. He finds fault with everything—what my mom cooks, what my dad says, what my brother thinks. And he's hardly subtle about it! And then I know I'll be criticized for everything they say and do as soon as we get home. Every goddamn time he has to come out with some shitty underhand thing to say that puts everyone ill at ease. He spoils my enjoyment. As a result, I don't see them as often as I would like, and I'm beginning to hold it against him."

Tiphaine sighed and added through gritted teeth, "You don't know how lucky you are! No family to bother you!"

The words, clearly intended as a harmless throwaway comment, struck Laetitia like a knife. She turned a bloodless face to Tiphaine, who realized too late the awfulness of what she had just said.

"Oh my god, I am SO SORRY!" she exclaimed. "Forgive me, Laetitia, I can't apologize enough. I didn't think . . . oh god, I'm so horrible, I'm going to be beating myself up for days . . ."

Laetitia sat frozen, staring at Tiphaine, pain and confusion etched on her face.

"Don't look at me like that!" begged Tiphaine. "I spoke without thinking, I didn't mean it, it was just words."

Too choked with emotion to speak, Laetitia walked over to the sink. She leaned on it heavily with her back to Tiphaine.

"Can you leave me alone, please?" she eventually murmured between clenched teeth.

"Sorry?"

"Take Maxime and go home," Laetitia said in the same tone.

Tiphaine went over to Laetitia, gently took hold of her shoulders, and turned her around. Laetitia's cheeks were wet with tears.

"I miss them so much!" she sobbed.

Tiphaine, mortified, pulled her into a hug and apologized over and over.

"You have no idea what it's like to feel all alone," Laetitia wept, "with no family to help you, support you, share in your happiness, your doubts and struggles in life. Whenever I think about my parents, it's like an iron fist is tearing my heart from my chest . . . and to think they never even met David and their grandson . . . they would have loved them so much!"

"I know, I know," Tiphaine murmured, though she could not help but think that if Laetitia's parents were still alive, they would probably have their own disagreements and differences of opinion, like every other family.

Nor was Tiphaine sure, when Laetitia talked about her parents, that David would have met with their approval: an ex-con with no qualifications and a former drug habit was hardly the ideal son-in-law every good conservative Catholic couple dreamed of. The truth was that the more she thought about it, the more convinced she was that if Laetitia's parents were still around, they would never have let David within a mile of their precious daughter. But having already put her foot in her mouth, Tiphaine decided to keep her opinion to herself.

"We would have been so happy!" Laetitia concluded, blowing her nose on a Kleenex Tiphaine handed her.

Tiphaine nodded pensively and said, in one final attempt to console her friend, "But you *are* happy! That's all that counts, Laetitia! You and David love each other, you have a wonderful little boy, a lovely home . . . and we're here! Sylvain, Maxime, and I are your substitute family. You can count on us. We're not blood, but we are family."

Laetitia looked up at her friend, her eyes full of gratitude. The two women shared a long hug.

CHAPTER 12

Friendship is a source of strength no one can live without. Everyone needs friends as much as sustenance and sleep. Friendship is nourishment for the soul; it cheers our hearts, feeds our minds, fills us with joy, hope, and peace. Friendship is life's treasure and the guarantee of a certain kind of happiness.

At the next Friday happy hour, as everyone was winding down after a busy week, Laetitia found herself overcome with a wave of emotion, as sudden as it was unexpected. It was ordinary moments like these that turned out to be priceless in hindsight, for no apparent reason. Maybe simply because they were perfect. Tiphaine had just called the boys down from Milo's bedroom. Their meal was on the table—two plates of the Friday night spaghetti with ham and cheese that both of them adored: no vegetables, so no shouting, tears, or threats. David and Sylvain were enjoying a drink in the living room, teasing each other about something or other, as they often did.

Tiphaine shouted upstairs for the boys for the third time. They tumbled down the stairs into the dining room, hooting with laughter.

"What's so funny?" she asked, intrigued.

The question just made Maxime and Milo laugh harder. Every time they looked at each other they started again, caught up in a spiral of hilarity. David and Sylvain, drawn by the joyful sound, came in to find out what was going on. To no avail: the boys were still laughing so hard they couldn't speak.

"Aren't they silly!" said Sylvain, beginning to chuckle in turn.

It was hilarious watching the boys doubled over giggling. The laughter spilled from them like a waterfall. Soon the parents all joined in, with no idea of what was so funny to the boys. Milo and Maxime, seeing the adults join in, laughed all the harder.

Laetitia suddenly felt a vast wave of happiness, all the more sweeping because she was aware of it. What did it matter that she and David had no other family? Yes, fate had been cruel to them. But their family was here, in front of her, sharing in a moment of unalloyed joy whose strength lay in its very presence without a visible cause. Two children with an unbreakable bond, enjoying all the carefree innocence of youth. Milo was happy, and his boyish delight brought tears to her eyes. Glancing at her, the other adults thought she was crying with laughter. Why did she think she was alone? Why complain? After all, Tiphaine and Sylvain both had families, and they didn't seem to be any happier for it . . .

Laetitia thought back to how resentful she had been the weekend before when Tiphaine made the clumsy reference to her lack of family. Looking back, she felt bad about it. She should not have been so inflexible with her closest friend, the woman she shared everything with except a blood bond. Her more than sister.

Gradually, the laughter died away and the evening got back on track. Later, after tucking the boys into bed, Laetitia looked for a scrap of paper before heading back downstairs. She scribbled two words: "Forgive me." Only around midnight, as Tiphaine was helping her clear the table before heading home with Sylvain, did she find an opportunity—and the courage—to slip her the note. Intrigued, Tiphaine unfolded the scrap of paper. She read the message, then looked up in surprise. "Forgive you? What for?"

"I know, it's stupid!" Laetitia was already apologetic. "It's about last weekend, I feel bad about making you feel bad."

"Are you nuts?"

Laetitia smiled. "It's good to say sorry when you were in the wrong."

"But *I* was wrong! *I* should be apologizing to *you*!"

"We could go on like this for a while!"

They burst out laughing. Then, not quite managing to master her emotions, Tiphaine carefully folded her friend's note and put it away in her pocketbook.

CHAPTER 13

The following Sunday, when Laetitia woke up, it wasn't due to wan light struggling through the blackout curtains nor the alarm on her cell phone, usually set to ring at 6:45 a.m. Torn from sleep with the unpleasant sensation that it was far too early to be awake, she reached out and felt blindly for her phone on the bedside table. Ten past seven. She nearly leaped out of bed to dash to the bathroom before wondering why the alarm had not gone off.

That was when she remembered—it was Sunday.

A dull thud from the other side of the wall told her what had woken her up on the one day she could enjoy sleeping in. She groaned in irritation and put the pillow over her head as another thud came through the wall. It was hard enough when Milo woke her up at seven on a Sunday morning. But when it was someone else's kid disturbing her precious sleep, it was enough to drive her nuts.

The noise was coming from Maxime's bedroom next door. Not only did he have the annoying habit of waking up at the crack of dawn on Sundays, but he made a lot of noise. She had already had a polite word with Tiphaine and Sylvain about it, and they had promised it would not happen again. Yet every

Sunday, Laetitia was brutally wrenched from sleep by Maxime's early morning antics. Today it sounded like he was playing soccer, aiming at the goalposts on the shared wall between their houses. Picturing the layout of his room, Laetitia realized there was little chance he would switch walls: the other three had bookshelves, a window, and a radiator on them. Meanwhile, David was still snoring away gently beside her, his steady, calm breathing irritating Laetitia even more.

For a brief moment, she was tempted to hammer on the wall, but she was not sure Maxime would get the message and stop kicking the ball. A series of goals accompanied by the distant echo of shouts of victory raised her exasperation to fever pitch: she would never get back to sleep now. She was fully awake. Laetitia got up, padded downstairs, and picked up the phone. On the eighth ring, a sleepy voice answered.

"Sorry to wake you, Sylvain," she declared abruptly. "Maxime is playing soccer in his room and it woke me up."

A brief pause while the information wound its way into Sylvain's half-asleep brain. "Oh, right. Sorry. I'll tell him to stop."

"Thanks."

She hung up and went to pee—she might as well—before returning to bed. Through the wall she could hear Sylvain telling Maxime off sharply and confiscating the soccer ball. Maxime protested vigorously, irritating Laetitia even more. After a few more shouts from Maxime and threats from Sylvain, all was quiet once more.

Laetitia sighed in relief and relaxed.

Milo, now six, struck with wonder on seeing the trace of a shooting star:

"Oh, a racing star!"

CHAPTER 14

When the fine weather returns after the long months of winter, it's like the burst of sunlight at the end of a long, dark tunnel. The horizon clears, our hearts grow warmer, our longings return, and we find ourselves torn between wanting to do a million things and doing nothing at all.

Nothing at all is exactly what Laetitia had planned for that afternoon. She fetched the deck chair from the shed and set it up facing the sun. She went back into the living room for a cushion, poured herself a cool drink in the kitchen, and picked up her book—a gripping mystery—from the bedroom. Once settled in the yard, she heaved a relaxed sigh. It was half past one. Three hours to call her own before she had to pick Milo up from school. Three hours of pure relaxation, when the only thing that would make her shiver was her spine-tingling thriller.

Fifteen minutes later, she was dozing in the gentle warmth of the spring sunshine. Overcome with delicious fatigue, she let the book slip from her fingers. It fell on the grass. Time stood still in a moment of beatitude. But the perfection of the moment was soon broken.

Something stirred Laetitia from her nap. No unusual noise,

no movement, only a feeling of vague dread. She opened her eyes, taking a moment to readjust and remember where she was, what time, what day it was. She sat up lazily, propped on her elbows, and looked around. The yard was as empty as when she had first sat down. The house seemed deserted too, but she called out just in case. "David? Are you there?"

She listened for him. He was on the day shift and wasn't due back until around five. Frowning, she looked all around, keeping her ears open. Nothing. She turned back to her book.

It was as she lay back down that he caught her eye. Just a glimpse. The unexpected presence of a little figure at the window. She immediately did a double take. From her vantage point in the garden, she could see the back of both houses. The hedge hid next door's terrace and ground-floor windows, but she could see the upper floor clearly. On the right, Tiphaine and Sylvain's bedroom. On the left, Maxime's.

And Maxime was leaning dangerously far out of the open window.

Laetitia leaped to her feet. She wondered briefly why he was at home on a school day, then remembered he was sick. Tiphaine had called her the previous day to ask if she had any cough medicine on hand.

"Laryngitis, the doctor said. We just have to keep his temperature down and give him the cough mixture if it keeps him awake at night. He gave us a homeopathy script—aconite, Spongia Tosta, and Hepar Sulph—but I've got all those. The cough syrup is the only thing I don't have in the house."

Tiphaine liked alternative remedies, generally treating her son with homeopathy and homemade herbal infusions. She knew a lot about medicinal plants from her time as a pharmacist and often used them at home. Laetitia was somewhat skeptical, but had to admit Maxime was rarely ill.

She approached the hedge so that Maxime could hear her. "Maxime! Get inside now!" she called, her voice sharp with anxiety.

"What?"

She realized in terror that calling out to him had had the opposite effect than intended. Rather than climbing back down inside, Maxime was now leaning out farther to hear her.

"Jesus Christ, Maxime! Get back inside now!" she screamed, waving her arms as if to push him back in herself.

"I'm hot," he moaned.

He was pale, his eyes ringed with dark smudges, and he seemed unsteady on his feet. Laetitia realized that his temperature was spiking and he had instinctively come to the window for some cool air.

"Christ, where's your mom? Tiphaine? Tiphaine!" she screamed across the hedge. Standing on her tiptoes, she could see the terrace door was open. For one interminable moment, she waited, hoping to see Tiphaine step out. But no. She looked back up at the window, choking back a cry of horror as fear filled her heart. Maxime was now leaning halfway out the window.

"I want my mom," he moaned, reaching his arms out to her.

Laetitia felt as if all the liquid in her body had suddenly frozen. In a flash of realization that seemed to last an eternity, she knew that if no one intervened in the next few seconds, something terrible was about to happen. She looked back up at Maxime, begging him with her eyes as she gestured futilely to him to get back inside. Her blood was frozen but her mind was racing, a thousand questions jostling in her brain: she had to act fast, do something, make sure it was the right decision. She screamed Tiphaine's name again, realizing as she did so that for some reason her friend could not hear her, and made up her mind to act. In a fraction of a second, she pulled herself together and ran into the living room. She dashed into the front hall, wondering for a precious second or two whether to grab the keys to next door—they had swapped keys for safekeeping—before deciding that the time lost looking for the key would be made up by unlocking the door herself without waiting. She snatched the drawer from the hallway unit, feverishly rifling through the tangle of useless junk collected over the years, desperately scrabbling for the keys. She couldn't find them, and her anxiety went up several notches. Swearing under her breath, she dropped the drawer and raced through the front door as if the house had spat her out. Within an instant she was mashing her finger on the Geniots' doorbell, long and loud.

"Who the hell is it?" shouted Tiphaine before finally coming to the door after several long seconds. She was in her bathrobe, her hair wrapped in a large pink towel: she had clearly just stepped out of the shower.

Her anger gave way to a look of puzzlement as she saw her neighbor on the doorstep. Laetitia rushed into the hall and up the stairs.

"Maxime! The window's open!" she screamed over her shoulder.

The four words reverberated through Tiphaine's brain,

triggering absolute horror. She screeched her son's name and shot up the stairs after her friend, taking the steps two at a time, hauling herself up by the banister, using all the strength of her hands and legs to propel herself up and past Laetitia.

Upstairs, the two women raced to the little boy's bedroom. The door was closed. Tiphaine was the first to grab the handle, throwing the door open with such force it crashed against the wall.

Then, silence.

The room was flooded with sunlight, casting the shadow of the curtains on the facing wall as they danced in the light breeze. The bedsheets were tangled. Empty. Like the window, a gaping maw opening onto the hell that Tiphaine and Sylvain's lives had just veered into.

Maxime was dead.

CHAPTER 15

A scream that lasted forever. A scream whose echo resonated for seconds that stretched to eternity, as if the merciless struggle between silence and sound could still the cruel hand of fate. A tsunami of stormy water smashing into the rigid wall of a dam, sending waves skittering endlessly across the surface, the current fading to the gentle ripple of a dying breath.

Laetitia leaned out the window. To be certain.

The image that branded itself on her retina as painfully as a red-hot iron told her there was nothing she could do.

Turning back, she saw Tiphaine's lost expression, her eyes wild with questions, with torment. Eyes screaming before the sound came spilling from her throat, a howl of horror, denial, and pain.

A howl that lasted forever.

And when it finally choked into silence—when her breath ran out, hiccupping in ragged jerks, when silence was on the verge of triumphing—awareness hit her anew, rubbing the unbearable truth raw. The scream bounced off the hollow, fleshy walls of a heart drained of its blood, echoing forever in the depths of a memory frozen in time.

Tiphaine stumbled over to the window. Laetitia grabbed her, pulled her back, trying to stop her from looking out.

Blue lights swirling outside the house. Men in white coveralls inside. White light, flat voices, hesitant movements that stopped and started again. Repeated over and over. Words hanging limply, pointlessly, in the air. Time of death: around two p.m.

Around . . .

Lonely numbers floating in an approximate sea, smashing each other to smithereens, dissolving into fragments, leaving only cruel solitude.

Maxime was dead.

The little body was carried away, shrouded in a halo of blue light from the ambulance. The neighbors stood watching from their doorsteps, arms crossed, shivering and whispering. Horror had just landed in their midst; death had brushed past their thresholds with its funereal pall. They shivered as the ambulance left, as if they had had a narrow escape. Whispering. "The boy at number twenty-six. Fell out of the window." "The one who's always sucking his thumb?" "No, that's the other one, number twenty-eight." "Yes, you know, the little blond boy, blue glasses, never says hello . . . I heard his mother was in the shower . . ."

When silence launches its attack, whispers become rumors, running wild, out of control, spreading breathlessly from loose lips to eager ears.

"Who died?" "The boy at number twenty-six. I heard the mother went out to buy some flour. Kid saw he was left alone, got scared, jumped out the window." "Real smart, leaving a six-year-old kid by himself!"

When words and numbers are gone, tears are all that remain. And silence. Now and forever. The silence of a missing presence screaming in your head, your heart, deep in your gut, leaving no peace, no respite, only the damp misery of regret.

"Kid wasn't even six yet, the mom left him alone, she's an alcoholic—I mean, come on, she went out on a bender and left the kid by himself for hours. Kid couldn't stand it any longer, killed himself."

Bitch!

"Why are you crying, Mom?"

Laetitia started in surprise, as if caught doing something she shouldn't. Without quite knowing how, she had found the strength to collect Milo from school, go through their daily routine, answer his trivial questions, ask him about his day, did he have a big lunch, was he a good boy today. She was on autopilot, and if you didn't look too closely, she could almost fake it. Keep up the façade just a little longer, because afterward, it was dawning on her, nothing would ever be the same again.

Tiphaine and Sylvain were at the hospital. Laetitia had no idea when they would be back. What should she tell Milo? Nothing for now. She didn't have the strength to mop up his grief when her own was so vast and so agonizing. Nor had she called David, fearing that the terrible news might cause him to crash. Terrified by the ferocious cruelty of life, she preferred to wait until he was home. Leave him a few hours' peace as well, maybe. Before his world also tipped over into the horror of the void.

In truth, Laetitia wanted to keep the before time for a few hours more—the time of carefree happiness when the only problems with their children were a lingering cough, or back talk with an insolent stare, or wrongdoings stubbornly un-confessed. The echo of her own complaints resonated in her thoughts: moaning with Tiphaine about everyday woes, sleep-less nights, telling the kids to brush their teeth ten times in a row, missing the late mornings of the preparenting years, fighting every day to get fruit and vegetables into children who rejected anything with vitamins in it.

Milo asked to go and play with Maxime as soon as they got home. He had missed his friend at school all day. He wanted to tell him about Solenne falling off the wall in the yard, scrap-ing her knee, and crying like a baby. And about the teacher telling Léon off for talking in class.

"Hey, Mom, can I go to play with Maxime?"

Laetitia was gazing into space. She stared at Milo without really seeing him. Gradually, the consequences of Maxime's death began to snake their long, tortuous tentacles into her mind, her thoughts, constricting around her heart, squeezing inexorably tighter. She could not shake off the viselike grip that would soon smother and choke her.

"Why are you crying, Mom?"

Laetitia wiped the tears from her cheeks with the back of her hand. She already knew that Milo would struggle to cope without Maxime. And that today, at around two p.m., a funeral bell had tolled, closing a chapter in their lives forever. The chapter of happy times.

CHAPTER 16

When David came home, Milo was splashing happily in the bath. Knowing that Milo could not sneak in and overhear them, Laetitia told him the whole story: sunbathing in the garden, Maxime leaning out of the window, her desperate attempt to ward off the catastrophe, the fatal fall. They both cried, clinging to each other. It was as if the little boy's death materialized as she told the story, becoming concrete, tangible. Irreversible.

Later, after Milo was in bed, still unaware of Maxime's death, David stepped out onto the terrace to sneak a look over the hedge. The lights were on next door: Sylvain and Tiphaine were home. He stood on tiptoe, craning his neck to see inside. He could make out several shadowy figures. Their two families must have come to visit after hearing the tragic news.

"I don't think this is a good time," he said, heading back into his own living room. "Better wait until tomorrow morning."

David was realizing just how strangely powerful tragedy was, how it could restore the hierarchy of human relationships. Tiphaine and Sylvain had been their closest friends for almost ten years, and he knew they were just as fond of him and Laetitia. The proof of their friendship was there every day, in all the mundane events that brought them closer and closer together. Sylvain had once confessed to him that he felt closer to David and Laetitia than to his own family. Yet all it took was one single event out of the ordinary, one single swerve off course, to put their biological family back at the top, above even the closest of friends. The power of the clan was formidable and blood bonds unbreakable. David could see it clearly, with a bitter twinge of sadness.

Sadness for the birth family he had hardly known.

Sadness for Laetitia's family, gone too soon.

Sadness for his own son, Milo, who had been cheated of the family bonds and problems that can forge or destroy us, but which either way keep us going.

Laetitia pulled herself out of her fog. "I need to see them," she murmured.

"I know." He took her in her arms. "But what you need doesn't matter right now. *They* matter. And what *they* need is to come together as a family, to grieve."

"I have to see Tiphaine," Laetitia moaned.

"Not tonight. The whole family is there. We would be in the way."

Laetitia nodded sadly. "What are we going to tell Milo?"

"The truth."

"When?"

"Tomorrow. We'll do it all tomorrow. For now, all we can do is cry."

So they cried, late into the night.

The next morning, they did what they had decided. David and Laetitia kept Milo home from school. They did not want to rush when breaking the terrible news to him.

Milo listened attentively, more intrigued by his parents' hesitancy than by the words themselves, which meant little to him.

"What does 'dead for good' mean?"

David and Laetitia exchanged a perplexed glance.

"It means he's gone to sleep forever," David reassured him.

"When will he wake up?"

Laetitia choked back a sob. "He won't wake up."

Milo was quiet for a while, clearly trying to grasp a reality that was too abstract for him.

"Where is he now?"

"For now he's at the hospital, but soon he will be buried at the cemetery."

"You mean he is going to sleep at the cemetery?" Milo exclaimed, his eyes wide with fear.

"Yes, that's where people go when they die."

"He can't go there! Maxime hates cemeteries, he told me so!"

"When did he say that?"

"One day. When he went to see Sylvain's grandpa."

Then he returned to the main question that was still bothering him. "Did it hurt when he fell?"

"Yes, a lot. But now he's not hurting at all."

"You mean he's all better?"

David could not suppress a sigh. "No, sweetheart. He's not all better. All better is when you're still alive. But one thing is for sure, Maxime is fine where he is, and he's not in pain."

Milo studied his parents, his gaze full of concern. Then, as if deciding that David's explanation was enough, his face relaxed.

"Can I watch TV?" he asked in an almost cheerful tone.

David and Laetitia looked worried.

"You do understand what's happened, don't you?" Laetitia asked in concern.

Milo nodded quickly.

"Can I, Mom? Please?"

"Let him get used to the idea in his own time," David suggested in a low voice. He turned to Milo. "What cartoon would you like to watch?"

"I thought the three of us were going over to visit Tiphaine and Sylvain," Laetitia whispered back.

"It's too soon for him!"

Aware that Milo was still drinking in every word, looking from David to Laetitia in curiosity, they stopped talking. After a brief, silent face-off, David came to a decision.

"Listen, kiddo. Your mom and I have to go see Tiphaine and Sylvain for a few minutes. It won't be fun for you because they are very, very sad. So what I suggest is I put on a cartoon for you, we put the baby monitor in the living room, and if you need anything at all, you just talk to the monitor, OK? We'll hear everything that happens here and we'll be right back. How does that sound?"

"Good!" Milo smiled broadly. While David tested the baby monitor, Laetitia went upstairs to check all the windows were closed. Then she checked her face and clothes in the hallway mirror. She didn't want to look too distraught: she had to be strong to help her friends. On the verge of breaking down sobbing even before setting foot next door, she fought desperately to master her emotions.

When David joined her in the hall, ready to leave, she stopped him for a moment.

"He took it too well, don't you think?"

"Who? Milo?"

Laetitia nodded. "He barely frowned," she added. "I mean, Maxime was almost a brother to him!"

"Milo is six. Death is too abstract for him to understand. You heard him, he doesn't even know what being dead means! He'll realize what it means that Maxime is gone gradually, in his own time. Right now, he can't cry about something he doesn't get."

Laetitia gave David a look of tender admiration. "Sometimes it sounds like you've got a PhD in psychology . . . Everything's so simple when you're here," she said, hugging him tight. "I don't know what I'd do without you."

He hugged her back. They stepped out of the hall and rang the bell next door.

Laetitia could not help thinking back to the last time she had reached out her index finger to press the button. Maxime was probably still alive. Now, standing on Tiphaine and Sylvain's doorstep in the exact same spot, she felt sick to her stomach.

Sylvain opened the door.

"My god . . . ," she murmured, seeing her friend's face etched with tormented agony.

Sylvain had aged a decade overnight. His eyes were hard yet lifeless, his jaw permanently clenched. His skin was gray. For once he was unshaven, and the stubble made him unrecognizable.

Seeing David and Laetitia on the doorstep, Sylvain stiffened. He stared at them for a moment, his eyes dark, without the slightest move to let them in.

Laetitia did not immediately pick up on the unease triggered by their visit. Overwhelmed with emotion, she threw herself into Sylvain's arms. He froze, lifting his arms a little as if touching her bothered him. Laetitia was lost in grief in his arms. Only long seconds later did Sylvain's icy stiffness and total lack of reaction strike her as odd. She pulled away, took two steps back, and stared at him in surprise.

"Hey, old friend," David mumbled. "We . . . we came by to see how you are doing."

"Badly," Sylvain said, shooting Laetitia a look filled with pain.

"Is Tiphaine in?" she asked, now clearly aware that something was wrong. Something other than Maxime's death.

Sylvain ignored her, turning to David. "We need to be alone for now. Sorry."

He shut the door without a word.

CHAPTER 17

David and Laetitia stood frozen outside the door for a long while. They were unable to speak or even move, so distressing was the torrent of incomprehension and grief raging through them. Eventually, Laetitia turned a distraught face to David.

"What's going on?" she stammered through her sobs. "Why . . . why don't they want to see us?"

"Come on, let's get back inside," David murmured, putting his arm around her shoulder.

Back inside . . . they couldn't! Laetitia's heart tore in two at the very thought of turning around and going back into her own house. She had been pacing around inside its four walls since the day before, feeling useless, saturated with loss and pity. She needed to do something. To keep active. Be there for them. Talk, hug, let her tears mingle with theirs, stand watch over their pain. Try, impossibly, to lessen their agony. Take things in hand. Find the soothing words hidden in her own heart, her gut, the innermost folds of her own suffering, like a game of hide-and-seek: counting to twenty to pass the time, hunting down the elusive emollient that would salve the monstrous wound, even for a second.

She wrenched herself away. "No! I want to know why they don't want to see us!"

"Sylvain didn't say he didn't want to see us," David explained. "He just said they need to be by themselves for now. We have to respect that. Come on, let's go back inside."

David's determination overcame Laetitia's torment. A couple of minutes after shutting their own front door they were back home, deeply shaken by their brief exchange with Sylvain.

Laetitia spent the next hour obsessing over the handful of words, playing over each movement, each sentence, each glance in her head. The more she thought about it, the more convinced she became that there was more to Sylvain's chilly attitude than grief.

There was something else. An idea kept hovering in the back of her mind: the corrosive inkling of a misunderstanding. Not being able to pin it down was driving her mad. A thousand times she picked up her phone to call Tiphaine, talk it out, swear eternal friendship . . . A thousand times she put it down again without dialing, conscious of the triviality of her own distress compared with the virulence of the devastation swamping her friend.

So for the first time since the tragedy, Laetitia thought back over what had really happened. The first thing that came to mind was a question, as simple to ask as it was frightening to answer: how could Tiphaine have left her six-year-old son alone in his bedroom with the window wide open?

Shattered by the thought, Laetitia sprinted to the toilets to vomit up what little food she had managed to choke down since the day before. Emptying her stomach brought her no relief, other than the sudden realization of what lay behind Sylvain's attitude. How could Tiphaine ever get over the intolerable guilt of causing her own son's death? Was it carelessness, negligence, fecklessness? Whatever had caused Tiphaine to be so remiss, Laetitia now knew that in her friend's eyes she was the sole witness to her culpable moment of forgetfulness. And now, for Tiphaine, Laetitia personified her own fateful failing.

How could anyone survive such an ordeal?

Despite the horror of her thoughts, Laetitia found some consolation in her newfound understanding. At least she now knew why Tiphaine and Sylvain didn't want to—*couldn't*—face them right now.

Once again, David was right. Time was the great healer. Let it do its work.

"Mom, can I go and play at Maxime's?"

Laetitia started. She turned to her son in shock, not knowing quite how to react to his innocent question.

"Milo, I . . . do you remember what Daddy and I told you about Maxime this morning?"

Milo looked down at his feet and mumbled a few words that she didn't catch. She gently lifted his chin and asked him to repeat himself.

"I didn't say I wanted to play *with* Maxime, I said *at* Maxime's," he said sulkily.

It was so unexpected that it threw Laetitia off balance. "I'm afraid that's not possible, sweetheart."

"Why not?"

"Because . . . because what happened yesterday made Tiphaine and Sylvain so sad they need to be alone. Do you understand?'

Milo burst out sobbing. Laetitia, herself on the verge of tears, hugged him tight, soothing his sadness with soft whispers.

"Cry, little man, let it all out," she murmured. "It helps, don't keep it all bottled up . . . "

She held him tight, wounded by his pain yet relieved to see him express his sadness at last. That morning, when they had broken the news of Maxime's death to him, she had been unsettled by his lack of reaction—almost disappointed that he needed no comforting.

Now, at least, she felt useful.

"We will all miss Maxime a lot," she continued, still hugging the sobbing boy tight. "And no one will ever take his place. But I promise you, sweetheart, over time, the big knot in your tummy will get smaller. And one day it will be gone completely. That doesn't mean you don't love Maxime anymore, it just means . . ."

"I don't have a knot in my tummy," Milo choked out between sobs.

"Not a proper knot, I mean, but I know it hurts. Me too, and Daddy. That's normal, sweetheart. We all loved Maxime very much."

"That's not why I want to play at his house," Milo said, wiping away his tears.

"Why, then?"

"I need to get Bunnikins."

"Bunnikins? Bunnikins is at Maxime's?"

Bunnikins, a cloth rabbit with long ears dressed in overalls and a baseball cap, was one of Milo's favorite stuffed animals. It wasn't the most precious or the most loved, but Milo was fond enough of it to make Laetitia close her eyes and sigh when he nodded.

The boys regularly loaned each other toys and had been forgetting them in each other's bedroom since they were old enough to take things next door. Nothing unusual about that. Until today, it had never mattered: if one wanted a toy or a stuffed animal back, the mothers just had to pick up the phone and, a few minutes later, the boy would have it back in his possession.

"I want Bunnikins," wailed Milo.

Laetitia could not see herself calling Tiphaine to fetch Bunnikins from her son's bedroom barely twenty-four hours after his death.

"Look, Milo, we will get Bunnikins back, I promise. But not today."

"But Bunnikins is MINE!" he raged, his little voice quavering as he stared at his mother in bewilderment.

"I know, sweetheart. But I really can't go and get Bunnikins now. You'll have to wait a little while."

Milo's chin began to quiver again, tears streaming down his cheeks, breaking Laetitia's heart all over again. She began to waver: *should* she call Tiphaine? Might Bunnikins be the excuse she needed to talk to her friend, storm the barricade of her suffering? Like a doctor setting a broken bone: painful but necessary.

"Calm down, sweetheart . . . ," she said, drying his tears. "I'll see what I can do."

Gathering her courage, she picked up the phone.

Then, slowly, she dialed Tiphaine and Sylvain's number.

Hearing the first rings, she felt a dull surge of panic rising. What would she say to her friend? What words to choose? How could she justify wanting to thrust herself on them, with an obstinacy verging on harassment?

The rings kept coming, all identical, all indifferent, spinning out Laetitia's nightmare. Her heart pounding in her chest, she realized she was as terrified of hearing Tiphaine's voice as of her silence. They were home, she knew they were, and the knowledge added to her torment.

After twelve rings, it switched to voice mail.

CHAPTER 18

Standing frozen, phone in hand, Tiphaine stared blindly at the name on the screen: Laetitia. The strident ringing tore through the silence that hung over the house like a pall. A silence more implacable still than the earsplitting insistence of the telephone.

Each ring was a sharp blade, a dagger through her heart. A series of electric shocks, each draining her of blood. Each ring hurled her deeper into the abyss of the hostile universe where she was now held prisoner. How could she find the strength to tread the earth when its most beloved creature had deserted it forever?

Never had she imagined that mental anguish could be so physically painful.

Don't think. Sweep away the words, ideas, images swirling endlessly in the infernal dance of pitiless affliction. Push back the realization of an unspeakable truth for another second. Don't speak. Don't move. Hold on to the illusion of purpose for a few seconds. And when those seconds are over, start again, an infinite loop.

The telephone eventually fell silent. Then, as if its sound were the strings holding a puppet upright, Tiphaine fell to the floor sobbing, surprised her wellspring of tears had not yet run dry.

CHAPTER 19

Time had never weighed so heavily on Laetitia, condemned to inaction. It was as if her anguish had transformed into molasses, gumming up every second and congealing her motions so they became difficult, almost painful. The various stages of the day felt jumbled, out of order, giving her the feeling she was doomed to roam aimlessly forever, surrounded by dead time—time killed by her own efforts to keep thinking, keep moving. But she couldn't start on anything, let alone think rationally and sensibly.

One thought obsessed her: she needed to be with Tiphaine. The rest melted away in odious, exasperating futility. Yet she also needed to look after Milo, who could tell his mother was distracted and was using every trick he could think of to catch her attention. His bad behavior and tantrums at long last got Laetitia through to the end of an interminable day.

The night was no more restful. In an uneasy dream, she saw herself back in Maxime's bedroom on the afternoon of the tragedy: the unmade bed, sunlight playing with the shadow of the curtains, the open window. Finding herself alone in the center of the room, some mysterious force propelled her to the window. She saw herself leaning out into the void, convinced she would see Maxime's broken body below. But instead of the little boy, it was a child-sized Bunnikins lying shattered on the terrace flagstones. Her initial reaction was one of vast relief until she turned and saw Milo huddled over, hiding his face in his hands, his body shaking with sobs.

The nightmare haunted her until dawn, when she finally sank into unrefreshing sleep. When she woke up, the absurd dream kept tormenting her. Fortunately, the morning rush chased away her demons, making room for much more prosaic concerns: get breakfast on the table, wake up Milo—he said he had slept well—get him dressed, and drive him to school.

Stepping into the school lobby, Laetitia held her breath: on an easel borrowed from the art room stood Maxime's photo, adorned with a black ribbon. Next to it was a table with an elegantly bound notebook in which people were writing notes of condolence. Several parents stood clustered around the improvised memorial, asking questions or talking in hushed voices about what they knew, or had heard. The school principal had done an excellent job: a psychologist would be coming to Maxime's class during the day to talk to them about the accident that had cost their playmate his life.

Milo's teacher, knowing the pair had been best friends, was waiting for him at the classroom door. After a few kind words, she turned to Laetitia to ask how he had taken the news of Maxime's death. Laetitia gave her a brief rundown, including his meltdown over Bunnikins.

"I almost felt that he missed Bunnikins worse than he did Maxime," she concluded, her voice full of pain.

"You shouldn't see it like that," the teacher reassured her. "Maxime's death is still abstract for him, but Bunnikins not being there feels very real. Realizing that his best friend is dead is too much for him to process right now—he's in self-protection mode. He's focusing on the missing toy to avoid thinking about his friend. It's easier for him. But we'll have to be particularly careful with him in the coming weeks. We'll have to help him grieve for Maxime. Not Bunnikins."

Laetitia nodded pensively, her nightmare still circling in her thoughts.

"Mrs. Brunelle," the teacher continued, "if I can ask . . . Maxime's parents have agreed to let us bring some of his closest friends to the funeral if they would like to be there. We need permission from the parents. The school will also be represented—I'll be there myself. And Milo . . ."

"Maxime's funeral?" Laetitia was taken aback. "Already?"

The teacher's surprise was obvious. "Maxime is to be buried at the local cemetery next Monday at ten. Didn't you know?"

Laetitia stared at the teacher, thunderstruck. The entire school knew something as crucial as the date and time of Maxime's funeral, and she—part of the child's closest circle—had no idea. Deeply upset, she nodded. She needed to get out of there.

"I imagine you'll be going to the cemetery as a family," the teacher continued, aware of Laetitia's discomfort and just as eager to bring the conversation to a close. "What I really need to know at this point is if you want Milo to be there, and if so, if he will sit with you or with his other friends from school."

Laetitia, unprepared, had no idea what to say.

"We need to plan ahead, you see, so we have to know how many children will need transport to the funeral. I'm sure you understand," the teacher insisted.

"We'll take Milo with us," Laetitia eventually stammered out. "We'll probably keep him at home the rest of the day."

The teacher nodded in silent acknowledgment. Then, as tactfully as she could, but with a certain sense of relief, she ushered Laetitia out and turned back to her class.

Outside, Laetitia faced the raging storm of questions whirling through her brain. Why hadn't Tiphaine and Sylvain given them the details about Maxime's funeral? What did it mean? Had they simply forgotten in their grief and pain? Or was it deliberate?

And if so, why?

Suddenly, their refusal of visits and even phone calls since the tragedy seemed to Laetitia to be clear signs of rejection. All the possible explanations she had come up with for Tiphaine and Sylvain's attitude fell away. She picked up her pace, dialing her office as she jogged along to warn them she would be late. Then she rushed—not home, but to the house next door.

CHAPTER 20

Tiphaine opened the door. When she saw Laetitia, she shrank into herself like an injured creature withdrawing into its shell. It was as if Laetitia had unwittingly triggered an invisible force field.

"What do you want?" Tiphaine's voice was barely a whisper.

Her defensive attitude confirmed Laetitia's worst fears.

"For God's sake, Tiphaine, what's going on? Why are you pushing us away?"

The question seemed to pain Tiphaine like an electric shock. Her face contracted convulsively. Before Laetitia realized what was happening, a torrent of pain and anger poured out of her.

"You want to know what's going on?" she asked, as though each word were a knife blade, slowly and meticulously gashing her skin. "My son is dead, Laetitia! My little boy, the person I love most in the whole world, the boy who made me a mother, is dead, and you almost saw it happen. Maybe you even did? How would I know? Where were you when he fell? Oh yes, I remember. You were sunbathing!"

The earth seemed to shake beneath Laetitia's feet, almost sending her reeling. When she regained her balance, she felt herself dragged under the roiling waves of a terrible tempest. For long seconds, she thought the hurt would never end.

"Have you gone crazy?" she exclaiming, trembling all over, eyes wide with shock. "How . . . how *dare* you blame me for what happened! I did everything I could to save him!"

"No, you didn't, Laetitia! What you did was leave him alone by the wide-open window! A six-year-old boy, alone, fifteen feet up in the air! And all you can think of is ringing the doorbell? Do you really think that was the best course of action?"

The blood drained from Laetitia's face as she gradually saw the hellish chasm opening up beneath her feet. Tiphaine was blaming her for Maxime's death. Her dearest friend, her most faithful ally, the closest thing she had to a sister, was accusing her of something she wouldn't wish on her worst enemy.

"I had to warn you!" she cried. The words sounded like a death rattle.

"No!" shouted Tiphaine, her eyes flashing with rage. "You had to stay with him to stop him falling! Talk to him, calm him down. Get him away from the window."

"I tried!" Laetitia snapped, vainly hoping Tiphaine would see reason. "But it made it worse! He just leaned out farther to hear what I was shouting!"

Laetitia could not believe it. Tiphaine's accusations had her rooted to the spot, dazed with shock and confusion.

"And how do I know it wasn't you ringing the bell like a madwoman that startled him and made him fall?" Tiphaine raved, not even listening to Laetitia.

"Tiphaine! You can't say that!"

"You should never have left him alone! You should have gone under the window to break his fall! If you'd done the right thing, he'd still be alive!"

"How could I? The hedge was in the way!"

Tiphaine's eyes lit up with a glimmer of madness. "How could you?" she screeched hysterically. "The hedge was in the way! Except instead of the damn hedge there should have been a gate, remember? A gate would have saved my son's life!"

Laetitia froze. Nothing she could say or do could convince her friend to see reason. In the brief silence that followed, Tiphaine's eyes were full of pain and rancor.

"I'm not saying it was all your fault," Tiphaine murmured, bursting into tears. "But one thing is for sure. You could have saved Maxime."

CHAPTER 21

Laetitia was no more than twenty feet from her own front door, but it seemed an unbridgeable gulf. Tiphaine had finished her furious accusations by slamming the door in Laetitia's face, leaving her alone on the doorstep, ravaged by bewildered anguish. For a brief moment she was tempted to hammer on the door in the violent hope of sparking a reaction from her friend, getting through to her, talking it out, even hurling hideous insults in each other's face. Anything but this unbearable sense of rejection.

Her last shred of dignity held her back.

She stumbled back home. Blinded by tears, she struggled to get the key in the lock. As soon as she found herself alone inside, she collapsed in the hallway. She lay there for hours. Or maybe a handful of minutes. Tiphaine's accusations swirled around her, murderous words echoing to infinity, bouncing relentlessly off the walls in the hallway and the bones of her skull.

"The hedge was in the way! Except instead of the damn hedge there should have been a gate, remember? A gate would have saved my son's life!"

If they had put in a gate like Tiphaine and Sylvain wanted,

could she have saved Maxime? Or was Tiphaine in so much pain that she could not picture the sequence of events rationally? Was she saving her own sanity by shifting the blame? Sensing a grain of truth in this last thought, Laetitia tried to hang on to it, but the virulence of her friend's attacks won out. The thought of her own guilt wormed its way into her, stirring a rising sense of panic that soon convinced her of her own indirect blame for the tragedy.

She crawled to the house phone in devastation, dialing David's cell. She was sobbing so hard it took him a few minutes to work out why she was in such distress.

"Don't move, I'm on my way!" he ordered before hanging up.

Fifteen minutes later, he rang Tiphaine and Sylvain's doorbell.

The confrontation was brief and pitiless. When Tiphaine opened the door, David demanded to be let in to clear the air.

"Leave us alone!" she moaned, closing the door on him.

But David was too quick for her. He slipped his foot in the doorway. "We have to talk!" he snapped in a tone that was harsher than he intended.

David's intrusion and sharp tone felt like an attack to Tiphaine. She stiffened defensively, casting him a ferocious, sneering look. "Move your foot, David, or I'll call the police."

"You'd do that?" he asked bitterly.

"Without a second's hesitation."

David gauged Tiphaine's rigid determination and saw that she was well past rational argument. He tried a different tack. "Where's Sylvain? I want to talk to him!"

Tiphaine's only response was to pull her cell phone from

her pocket and brandish it in his face. "If you haven't moved your foot in five seconds, I'm calling the police."

David stared at her, his bewilderment clear from his face.

"I know Maxime's death must be unbearable for you, Tiphaine, but . . . "

"Four."

"You cannot blame Laetitia for what happened," he continued, forcing calm into his voice.

"Three."

David gazed at her, his eyes filled with pain. Tiphaine held his gaze as if she were now a disembodied spirit, a curious onlooker watching someone else's argument. A few seconds later, she sighed and began dialing a number on her cell phone.

"Forget it, Tiphaine," David murmured, taking a step back.

She slammed the door, holding his gaze the entire time.

Alone on the sidewalk, David clenched his teeth as a wave of powerlessness washed over him, even more unbearable than Tiphaine's insane, baseless allegations. Looking at the problem from all angles, he instinctively grasped that there was nothing he could do right now other than go home to Laetitia, soothe her, calm her fears, draw out the poisonous sting of guilt that Tiphaine had planted in her mind.

He turned around regretfully.

Just before he opened his own front door, he glanced up at the Geniots' second-floor windows. Someone was standing motionless behind the left-hand window, half hidden by the curtain. It was Sylvain, and it was clear from the way he was standing that he was spying on David.

David took a step back onto the sidewalk to face Sylvain. For a brief second, he thought Sylvain might open the window and speak. But he didn't. Sylvain stood there for long seconds, unmoving, like a statue. The two men stared at each other, then Sylvain lowered his head. He took a step back and jerked the curtain shut.

CHAPTER 22

When Laetitia woke up, it wasn't due to wan light struggling through the blackout curtains or the alarm on her cell phone, usually set to ring at 6:45 a.m. Torn from sleep with the unpleasant sensation that it was far too early to be awake, she reached out and felt blindly for her phone on the bedside table. Ten past seven. She nearly leaped out of bed to dash to the bathroom before wondering why the alarm had not gone off.

That was when she remembered it was Sunday.

She raised one hand to her forehead and groaned. David was still snoring away gently beside her, his breathing steady and calm, irritating Laetitia even more. Why was she awake so early? All was calm, not a sound disturbing the serene tranquility of the early Sunday morning . . .

Suddenly she stiffened, realizing what had jerked her awake. The silence. Emptiness. The void.

Death.

Usually, what got her out of bed on Sundays was Maxime playing loudly in his bedroom just behind her head. That morning, it was an unbearable absence. No more hammering on the wall or calling up Tiphaine and Sylvain to tell their son to keep it down.

She had to force herself to lie there, her eyes wide open, aching with a sense of loss for the blessed days when Maxime played soccer in his bedroom at seven on Sunday mornings, kicking his ball at the wall over and over again.

CHAPTER 23

David and Laetitia wavered for a long time about Maxime's funeral. Would it be decent for them to attend? On the one hand, Tiphaine and Sylvain's attitude had clearly shown them they would not be welcome, especially since they had not even been invited. On the other hand, if they missed it, people might gossip about Laetitia's involvement, which was totally unfair.

David thought they should attend with their heads held high, without provocation but with dignity. Laetitia worried that their presence would cause a scene. She was no longer sure of anything, especially Tiphaine's mental health. The question was tricky since Milo would be there, and neither David nor Laetitia wanted him to see his godmother ranting and raving. How would he react if Tiphaine forced them to leave? How would they explain they were no longer on speaking terms after being such close friends for so long? On top of that was their own immense sense of bereavement: they had seen Maxime as a newborn, growing, developing, blossoming. They had a deep attachment to him, loved him almost like their own son. Missing his funeral was simply unthinkable.

Their love for Maxime tipped the balance. They would attend.

So they did: David in defensive mode, Laetitia in a daze. Milo's teacher had given them the details. The ceremony would take place at ten at the funeral parlor, where Maxime's family and friends would come to say one last goodbye. Walking through the doors, Laetitia had to force herself not to look for Tiphaine. The last time she had attended a funeral, it was for her own parents, and the solemn atmosphere gripped her throat as soon as she stepped inside. Her heart started pounding in her chest so violently that she slowed down. David, following closely behind her, pressed her lightly on the back to keep walking. She tried to melt into the crowd as fast as she could, hoping valiantly not to be noticed. When she reached the opposite side of the group, she stopped.

"Keep going," David whispered in her ear. "Closer to the casket."

She instinctively shook her head, unable to take a single step more.

"Keep going!" he urged.

"I can't," she moaned, turning to him with eyes filled with anguish.

David grabbed her by the wrist, stepped in front, and pulled her along behind him. She let herself be dragged along, Milo close behind her. When they were near the front, David spotted three empty chairs. They sat down.

The room was dominated by the casket, its tiny child-sized proportions overwhelming the space with sadness. Laetitia was stirred to the depths of her soul when she saw the casket was open, showing the little body frozen in his last pose. Dressed in a dark suit, Maxime lay serenely still, hands crossed on his chest, eyes closed, his features relaxed. He could almost have been asleep. The sight of Maxime sent Laetitia's head spinning. She leaned heavily on David's shoulder. He looked at her with concern.

"I'm OK," she whispered after a long sigh.

"You just need to hold it together a little longer," he murmured.

She nodded, smiling wanly, before turning back to Maxime.

She hadn't seen him since the afternoon of the tragedy. Not seeing his body earlier, not weeping over it, had made his death almost abstract. Now seeing him in front of her, almost within arm's reach, pale, stiff, lifeless, tore her heart in two. Tears spilled uncontrollably from her eyes, her body shaking with irrepressible sobs.

Next to her, David wept silently.

Laetitia focused on the casket, striving desperately to soothe her own anguish. Through her tears, she could dimly make out Tiphaine and Sylvain by the coffin, but she dared not look straight at them. Their presence etched itself on her retinas, drawing her gaze like a pitiless siren song. She could stand it no longer: she turned her head slightly, catching Tiphaine staring at her with such distress that Laetitia had to struggle to keep standing. She forced herself not to look away, terrified by the thought that Tiphaine might break out in hysterics.

Nothing happened. After a few interminable seconds,

Tiphaine dropped her gaze, releasing Laetitia from a thousand torments. Only then did she allow her sorrow free rein.

The ceremony began. Sylvain's brother read a text about a life cut short, the unfairness of Maximes's early death, the pain of his loss. His voice was shot through with sobs that he tried to choke back in vain. Then it was Sylvain's mother's turn to say a few words, which she addressed to the tiny body in the casket, describing their relationship, her love for the little boy, and his hopes and dreams.

"You wanted to be a pilot," she said. "I want to believe you didn't fall. No! You flew! I know now you grew wings and are now flying in heaven. Your dream came true, sweetheart."

"A pilot?" whispered Laetitia. "Maxime never said anything about being a pilot!" Bitter realization dawned on her that the old woman describing Maxime with such assurance knew next to nothing about the boy.

"He doesn't want to be a pilot, he wants to play soccer!" Milo declared loudly.

Maxime's grandmother looked unsettled. A few scattered nervous laughs rose from the rows of seats. Laetitia shushed Milo, thinking of the old saying, "Out of the mouths of babes . . ." She realized that Milo had used the present tense, as if in his mind Maxime was still alive.

Other people stepped up to speak: Tiphaine's mother, her sister, Maxime's teacher. One of his cousins played a tune on the guitar. Then, at Tiphaine and Sylvain's request, the loudspeakers played the theme tune from *SpongeBob SquarePants*, Maxime's favorite cartoon. The cheerful tune and comic lyrics formed a striking contrast with the solemnity of the moment. Many people were weeping openly.

The emotion reached a crescendo when Sylvain stood up to speak. He began by saying he was also speaking for Tiphaine, as he was sure people would understand that she was not up to talking in public. After a long silence, when the attendees began to wonder if he was able to speak himself, he cleared his throat and began. Like his mother had done, he spoke directly to his son, telling him he loved him to the moon and back, that his birth had changed everything, had showed him what it meant to be a father. Showed him what really *mattered* in life. He talked about their fabulous, miraculous, rare, magical, intense, irreplaceable family of three, how they had learned more about one another every day and nourished their family unit with the deepest of love.

The entire room was holding its breath, tears flowing freely. Then Sylvain broke. He stepped over to the casket, stroking his son's head with infinite tenderness, and wept for long seconds, murmuring his goodbyes.

The funeral was drawing to a close. A discreet sign from the director indicated that anyone who wished to approach the casket for a final farewell could do so. People stood up and began to file toward the center of the room. David, Laetitia, and Milo took their places in the line. When it was their turn, Laetitia hoisted Milo up onto her hip so he could take one last look at his friend. She hoped that if he saw Maxime's lifeless body, he might at least understand the finality of his death.

The three of them stepped up to the casket together. Maxime lay peacefully on the padded white silk lining. His parents had placed his favorite toys all around him. A toy truck, a car, a SpongeBob figurine, and two stuffed animals . . .

"Bunnikins!" screamed Milo, the word tearing through the atmosphere of solemn mourning.

Laetitia started in surprise. Without thinking, she slapped her hand over his mouth, hissing at him to be quiet. Then, realizing what had triggered Milo, she looked down at the toys in Maxime's casket.

One of them was Bunnikins.

She dropped her hand from Milo's mouth in surprise. He exclaimed, loud and clear, "That's Bunnikins! Bunnikins is *mine*!"

And he leaned down to grab the cuddly toy.

Still clutching Milo in her arms, Laetitia just had time to take a step backward to stop the ultimate sacrilege.

"That's *my* bunny!" Milo roared. "I want my Bunnikins!"

David tried to reason with him, but he was not listening. He reached out for the cuddly rabbit, struggling in his mother's arms, crying "Bunnikins! Bunnikins!" over and over again. Laetitia, more and more flustered, stepped back from the casket, trying to calm her son down. But the more she stepped back, the angrier Milo got, thumping and kicking at her as he tried to wriggle free.

Everyone around them was murmuring in horror.

Laetitia wavered, not knowing what to do. In her dismay, she locked eyes with Tiphaine, now standing in front of the casket as if to keep everyone at bay. Tiphaine was staring at her, her eyes wild and threatening. Laetitia rushed for the exit, staring blindly ahead. Milo was still shouting, his body stiff as a board as he reached desperately for the casket, making it harder for Laetitia to carry him. He was nearly slipping from her arms. Exhausted, she loosened her grip for a second or two. Milo wriggled free, sliding down her legs, and ran toward the casket.

David grabbed him, threw him over his shoulder, grasped Laetitia by the hand, and made for the exit.

They ran out like a pair of thieves.

CHAPTER 24

Laetitia held it together until they were in the car. David strapped Milo, still in the grip of a tantrum, into his car seat. His screaming pierced through Laetitia until she lost her cool completely. Sitting in the front seat, she screamed in turn, making Milo freeze in terror. It was not subtle, but it worked. Milo instantly stopped yelling. She turned to face him, screeching like a banshee in anger and humiliation.

"Do you realize what you did in there!" she yelled, her eyes wild with rage. "You behaved like a spoiled brat at your best friend's funeral! Everyone was staring at us! You brought shame on me, Milo. I will never forgive you!"

"Calm down, Laetitia!" ordered David, horrified by her language.

"It was Bunnikins!" Milo raged, bolder now he felt his father was on his side. "He's mine! He's *my* bunny!"

"SO WHAT!" roared Laetitia, ignoring David. "Who cares about your stuffed animal! Maxime is *dead*, do you hear me? He's gone forever, it's over, you'll never see him again! Do you get that? Do you?"

"That's *enough*!" David said again. But it was as if Laetitia were deaf.

"And don't go thinking he's floating around somewhere in the sky, looking down on us with eyes full of love and tenderness! That's bullshit, his grandmother just wants to believe that so she won't be following him into the grave. There's no more Maxime, in the sky or anywhere else!"

"That's not true!" wailed Milo, terrified by his mother's behavior. "He's not gone, he was just there, sleeping in that funny bed!"

"No, he wasn't sleeping!" she screamed, on the verge of hysteria.

"Laetitia!" David yelled to make her shut up. Milo hid his face in his hands, as if to protect himself from his screaming mother.

"Look at me, Milo!" Laetitia roared. "Look at me when I'm talking to you!"

He reluctantly looked up at her, his eyes full of rage, jaw clenched and brow furrowed.

"Maxime was not asleep," she said icily, uttering each syllable clearly. "The funny bed was a casket. And in a few minutes, he'll be buried in the cemetery. They will put him in the ground. And he will stay there forever!"

"Jesus Christ, will you shut up?" David yelled. "Have you lost your goddamn mind?"

"He needs to understand, David!" she hissed, turning to face him at last. "He needs to know that was the last time he would see Maxime!"

"He *knows* that!"

"No, he doesn't! He still talks about him in the present, as if nothing had happened!"

"It's too much for a little boy to process. We've just got to give him time."

"Time? What for? To imagine things that aren't real? To believe his own lies, because it's easier than facing the truth? He keeps going on about Bunnikins, as if the damn rabbit counted more than Maxime!"

"He's trying to protect himself!"

"Yes, and that is exactly what I don't want! It's up to us to protect him, David, we can't leave it up to him!"

Laetitia's last point threw David off guard. Not knowing what to say, he stared at her in silence, then nodded imperceptibly.

"OK. But screaming at him isn't protecting him. You're doing it all wrong, Laetitia. And now is not the right time. We're all on edge."

Laetitia nodded back. The three of them were silent for a while. Milo, who had not spoken while his parents argued, was now eyeing them suspiciously. David turned to him with a weak smile. Milo burst into tears.

Laetitia, mortified, slid onto the back seat and took him onto her lap.

"Why are you crying now?" she asked gently, sure the enormity of Maxime's death had now struck him.

"I don't want Bunnikins to be buried with Maxime in the cemetery!" he wailed. David and Laetitia exchanged a worried look. David seemed to come to a decision. He put on his seat belt and told Laetitia to strap Milo in again, then herself. He turned the key in the ignition and sped off.

"Where are we going?" Laetitia asked, intrigued.

"To buy another Bunnikins."

CHAPTER 25

A couple of minutes later, they parked outside the biggest toy store in town. Milo was all smiles again and strode proudly along the aisles like a king, followed by his parents. The shelves overflowed with all kinds of toys: brightly colored baby toys, wooden cubes for building towers, shape sorters, miniature farms with tiny livestock, dollhouses, puppet theaters, books that played music, and jigsaw puzzles. A couple of aisles farther on were board games, educational games, and electronic toys for older children, alongside an incredible range of figurines from films and TV series: Transformers, Pokémon, Star Wars, Dragon Ball Z, and American wrestlers for boys; Barbie, Strawberry Shortcake, Hello Kitty, and Dora the Explorer for girls.

When they came to the stuffed animals, David turned to Milo:

"Here you go. You can choose whichever one you want."

All sorts were on display: plump, long and thin, short and stout, soft, funny, colorful, furry. Some were designed to look like pets, others were some outlandish alien species.

"Even a very big one?" Milo asked cautiously, unable to believe his luck.

"Even a very big one! As long as we can fit it in the car," David added, ruffling his hair.

Milo couldn't believe it. He ran his eager gaze over the dozens of stuffed animals on display and sighed with happiness. His first pick was a medium-sized rabbit in overalls and a baseball cap, like Bunnikins. Then he changed his mind. He put the rabbit back and headed straight for a giant, soft teddy bear with a friendly smile.

"This one!" he announced, turning to his father.

"You're absolutely sure?"

Milo nodded vigorously.

"Fine, that's settled!" David declared. He picked up the bear and held it out to Milo, who grabbed it, his eyes wide with delight. David strode energetically toward the cash register, accompanied by a triumphant Milo. Laetitia followed them a few steps behind, torn between the consolation of her son's beam of delight and the intuition that it would take more than a new toy to solve the big problems that lay ahead. But her guilt for the way she had screamed at him was too strong. For now, all that mattered was Milo's smile and the gleam in his eye.

When they left the store, she laughed. "A big bear called Bunnikins . . . that's funny, isn't it?"

"He's not called Bunnikins!" Milo retorted.

"Oh, really? What are you going to call him, then?"

"Maxime!" Milo said happily, clutching his new teddy bear tight.

CHAPTER 26

They spent the rest of the day at home, trying to relax. The morning had been too emotionally intense and both David and Laetitia were eager for a moment of calm, without clashes and conflict. Milo played with the new teddy in his bedroom for a good half hour, then Laetitia read him some stories and they did some drawings together. Both steered clear of talking about Maxime and the funeral. They threw together some pasta for lunch, which Milo wolfed down. He was the only one with any appetite. After lunch, David and Milo settled down to watch cartoons on TV and Laetitia sat outside on the terrace. The weather was gorgeous. The sun shone in a cloudless sky, a light breeze mitigating the heat.

She drifted off for a while. After twenty minutes, she was woken by snatches of conversation, chairs being moved around, glasses clinking. The Geniots next door were back from the funeral and their closest friends and family were there for the wake.

Laetitia suddenly felt ill at ease. Like an illicit eavesdropper. Out of place. A spy. She could overhear their conversations and glimpse them moving through the hedge, an unwilling witness to a private moment she had not been invited to. "This is my home!" she muttered, trying to convince herself she was doing nothing wrong. Yet it felt inappropriate to stay outside. Instinctively, she got up as quietly as she could and tiptoed inside.

As if trying to hide her presence.

The incident disturbed her. For the first time since moving in, living so close to the neighbors bothered her, prevented her from enjoying her own yard. Her heart sank as she thought that on top of the anguish caused by the week's events and finding themselves at daggers drawn with their—former?—friends, living next door was not going to make things easy. Worse yet, she felt her own privacy was being violated. If she could see and hear everything happening next door, they could certainly see and hear her family too. The low voices murmuring in next door's garden suddenly felt aggressive: she felt naked and exposed to people who wished her ill.

The thought kicked her stress levels up a notch. How could the two families carry on living side by side? Bumping into each other in the street, seeing each other come and go, catching sight of each other in their back gardens? There was too much history to just ignore everything they had shared—a deep friendship, so many shared joys, and now the boundless anger that Tiphaine and maybe even Sylvain had for them . . .

For an instant, Laetitia wished with all her heart that they would move out. And after all, why wouldn't they? How could they carry on living in the house where their little boy had died?

Would they be able to walk past his bedroom every day, past the window that caused the worst tragedy any parent can face?

"Finished your nap already?" David asked in surprise, still slouched in front of the TV.

"I'm going up to take a shower," replied Laetitia, unwilling to share the real reason she had come back in.

She headed upstairs.

Late that afternoon, something unexpected happened. Milo was in the bath, David was cooking, and Laetitia was cleaning upstairs when the front door bell rang.

"Can you get that?" David called upstairs. "I'm in the middle of cooking."

Laetitia headed downstairs and opened the door.

She held back a startled cry. It was Tiphaine and Sylvain. Her defenses immediately went up: she took a step back and turned her head, as if judging how far away David was in the kitchen.

"It's OK, Laetitia, we're not here to blame you for anything," were Sylvain's first words, holding up his hands in a conciliatory gesture. Laetitia, more and more taken aback, stared at them wordlessly.

"Can we come in for a minute?" he almost begged.

As if to demonstrate that they had not come to fight, Tiphaine pulled something from her bag. Laetitia recognized it immediately.

"We've come to give this back to Milo," she mumbled, holding out Bunnikins.

Laetitia, still dumbstruck, reached out for the toy blankly. They stood there mutely staring at each other for a few seconds, then Laetitia seemed to recover from her shock and stepped aside to let them in.

When David saw them in the living room, his reaction was more or less the same as Laetitia's. He froze, dropping the wooden spoon dripping with white sauce, opening his eyes wide in astonishment.

"What the hell are you doing here?" he demanded, his tone more aggressive than he meant.

"It's fine," Laetitia reassured him softly. "They came to give Milo Bunnikins."

"And to apologize," added Sylvain.

Laetitia turned to him, her expression even more thunderstruck than when she had opened the door. Sylvain turned to Tiphaine: clearly, she had something she needed to say.

A heavy silence hung over the room. Tiphaine seemed lost in an abyss of pain. She stood there like a statue, unmoving.

"Tiphaine?" Sylvain murmured, taking her hand.

She quivered, seeming to wake from a nightmare, then looked at David and Laetitia in surprise.

"Are you OK, sweetheart?" Sylvain asked anxiously.

"Why don't we all sit down?" suggested David, hoping to lighten the atmosphere.

"Can I get you something to drink?" Laetitia added hurriedly.

She headed for the kitchen, but Tiphaine intercepted her. Laetitia turned to face her, dumbfounded. Then, as if her strength had given out, Tiphaine fell into her arms and wept until her tears ran dry.

"I'm so sorry," she sobbed, distraught. "I've been horribly unfair to you. But it hurts so bad, if only you knew . . ."

"I know," Laetitia said quietly, hugging her friend tight.

CHAPTER 27

They talked, and cried, for a long time. Laetitia felt she had never shed so many tears in her life, not even when her own parents died. They had spoken in the last five days only to spit angry words, so it felt strange to return to terms that were polite, if not exactly friendly: David and Laetitia were still on their guard, thrown off by the sudden about-face.

Tiphaine and Sylvain were a mere shadow of their former selves. Both sat slumped, their eyes dull, the only spark of emotion the occasional flash of deep anguish and unbearable distress. Every now and then one of them would leave a sentence unfinished, eyes lost in the distance, and when David or Laetitia cleared their throat to bring them back or asked them to go on, the thread was broken, the thought long gone.

At long last, they came to the circumstances of Maxime's death. In a toneless voice, Tiphaine told them how Maxime's temperature had shot up to 103 degrees in the afternoon. She had given him some Advil to bring down the fever and put him to bed. He dozed off immediately, but Tiphaine stayed sitting with him for a good fifteen minutes. It was hot in the bedroom. The sun shone directly on the window. Beads of sweat formed on Maxime's nose and forehead, so she pulled back the covers and opened the window to let some fresh air in. His breathing grew more regular and he seemed to be deeply asleep, so she stepped out of the room for a quick shower.

That was all. She just wanted a quick shower.

When the story was over, she fell silent, her head bowed, shoulders slumped. The only sign that betrayed her devastating inner turmoil was the frenzied wringing of her hands.

David, Laetitia, and Sylvain said nothing.

In the end, Laetitia was the first to speak. She told them how things had happened from her point of view, while Tiphaine was in the shower. She gave a blow-by-blow account, leaving out just one detail: she could not tell her friend that in the grip of fever, Maxime had called out for his mom. There was no point twisting the knife in Tiphaine's wound. She simply said she had seen the little boy leaning dangerously out the window, calling to her, but she couldn't make out his words. The rest of her account was the strict truth.

Then, hoping to settle the point of contention that had torn them apart since the tragedy, she asked them point blank, "Do you think I could have saved him?"

Sylvain replied, "You did everything you could, Laetitia."

She nodded pensively. Strangely, that was not the response she was hoping for.

Suddenly, she remembered that Milo was still in the bath. The water must have long since gone cold. She dashed upstairs and pushed open the bathroom door. Milo was not there.

The ground opened up beneath her feet.

"Milo!" she shrieked, in the grip of panic.

She raced out of the bathroom and into Milo's bedroom. He was fast asleep on the bed, wrapped in a large towel, clutching his new teddy bear. In the meantime, David, Tiphaine, and Sylvain had rushed upstairs, alerted by her shriek, and were now crowded in the corridor behind her.

"It's fine, everything's OK," she mumbled. "He's asleep."

"Are you insane, screaming like that?" scolded David. "I almost had a heart attack!"

"Sorry. I was scared. I went into the bathroom, he wasn't there, and I thought . . ." She left the words hanging in the air. Almost automatically, her gaze was drawn to Tiphaine, who looked at her with such pain in her eyes that Laetitia flushed with shame. Shame about having screamed, shame about her own fear.

Shame about having a living son.

Taking her eyes off Laetitia, Tiphaine began walking toward her. One step and then another. Laetitia instinctively retreated, as if seeking protection. But Tiphaine kept going, past her, and into Milo's bedroom. She walked over to his bed and knelt down beside it. Then, infinitely tenderly, with a feather touch, she stroked his cheek.

Laetitia felt a strange knot forming in her stomach. She had to bite her tongue not to order Tiphaine out of the room. The words *don't touch him!* were on the tip of her tongue, ready to spill from her lips, as if her friend were somehow a threat to the little boy. Ridiculous! Tiphaine was Milo's godmother. She loved him, Laetitia knew she did. So where was her sense of latent danger coming from?

Suddenly, Laetitia felt her eyes drawn to Milo's new toy. Maxime!

A chill ran down her spine. Her heart leaped into her throat at the thought that Milo might wake up and tell Tiphaine the name he had chosen for his teddy bear. She stepped into the room, stopping just behind Tiphaine.

"Let him sleep," she suggested, keeping her voice deliberately calm. "He's exhausted after all today's emotions. He needs to rest."

Tiphaine nodded and stood up, not taking her eyes off the child for a second.

Then everyone headed back downstairs.

CHAPTER 28

The days passed.

As they must.

Life went on, under duress. Tiphaine and Sylvain got out of bed through sheer force of habit, ate when they happened to remember, kept themselves alive more by luck than design. Time had crumbled into a sort of shapeless maze with no way out. So what was the point of going on? Their lives, which from now on would be lived in an empty no-man's-land, seemed right now like they were part of a falsified reality that was no better or worse than any other.

Take it or leave it. What's the difference?

On the scale of mental pain, there comes a point where the anguish is so intense it seems delusional to think it will ever lessen. Stripped of any semblance of normality, the couple seemed to be barely surviving, as if exiled from a life shattered into shards so small they couldn't even be seen. What absurd reason could make them want to pick up the pieces?

Their hearts were broken beyond repair, their souls destroyed.

For David and Laetitia, time's wheel began to turn once more. Slowly, joylessly, mechanically. They carried out their daily routine: get up, eat, go to work, go to sleep . . . or rather lie awake. Strangely, ever since Tiphaine and Sylvain had stopped blaming her, Laetitia felt a deep, pernicious wellspring of guilt that focused obsessively on a single question: could she have done more to save Maxime? The poison of Tiphaine's blame coursed through her all night. Tormented by a waking nightmare, she ran through the tragedy again and again, forcing herself to do something different each time. To begin with, she ran to the back of the yard to wriggle through the hole the boys had made in the hedge. Then she raced up Tiphaine and Sylvain's yard to the house. She was too late every time. Maxime lay broken on the terrace.

Then she tried something new. She wriggled through the hedge faster, then dashed over to the window to catch the child as he fell. To no avail: when she got there, the little body lay sprawled on the chilly flagstones.

One night, she tried a new method of rescue, dragging a chair over to the hedge to climb over, shaving off a precious few seconds. Success! She made it to Maxime's window before he toppled out. But she could never catch him as he fell. He smashed heavily to the ground beside her, and the sound of his fall tortured her until dawn.

After a week, she gave up on the absurd, vain attempts. Her sleepless nights grew pale, diaphanously wan, as she lay there, wordlessly staring up at the darkness, sinking at long last into dreamless sleep for a few short hours before she had to wrench herself from her bed, choke down some breakfast, and head out to work.

Was it guilt that drove Laetitia to drop by next door after

work each day, just before she picked Milo up from school? It was clear that the tragedy and Tiphaine's slanderous accusations had damaged their relationship. Of course, Laetitia immediately chalked Tiphaine's reaction up to her deranged grief . . . but even so! The episode had corroded their friendship, leaving Laetitia with a sense of suspicious vigilance that she could tell had eaten away at their mutual trust. The way Tiphaine had totally shunned her in the immediate aftermath had desecrated her own pain, twisting her own legitimate grief into a more awful torment.

By blaming her for Maxime's death, Tiphaine had stolen from her the dignity of mourning.

Laetitia knew that there were extenuating circumstances to weigh in the balance, but she nonetheless felt a vague rancor.

That was probably why her daily visits never lasted very long. She would drop in for half an hour, see how they were getting on, ask if they needed anything. Anchoring their days with a friendly visit. And talking about Maxime. Laetitia forced herself to say his name. She had read online that mourning a child was inevitably a long, painful process, but it would never be completed if everyone conspired to bury the memory of the loss in the silence of grief. It was damaging to try to heal the soul's wounds by leaving the source of the pain unspoken. She quickly understood that the only thing stopping her friends from sinking into the void of their now meaningless lives was the memory of their son. Taking those memories from them would have been unspeakably cruel.

Tiphaine and Sylvain opened their doors to her neither gladly nor unwillingly. Some days it was a useful duty, others a necessary evil. There was no question of them fighting it, let along moving on. Pain was all that gave them the strength to keep moving, stumbling blindly toward a nonexistent future. They owed it to themselves to hurt, to feel the agony of Maxime's absence, to endure the torture as irrefutable proof of their love for their child. Suffering was now their only reason for living.

Laetitia was acting on instinct. Often she would bring them messages of condolence from other neighbors and local storekeepers she bumped into around town, or from the teachers and parents who asked after them at school and sent their warmest sympathies through her. She felt it was important for Tiphaine and Sylvain to know people were thinking of them. And, above all, that no one had forgotten Maxime.

Every time she stepped through their front door, the oppressive silence inside the house struck her like a whip, amplified by the couple's newfound habit of only talking in whispers, as if fearful of waking someone up. Murmuring, tiptoeing, moving around with tormented care. To begin with, Laetitia followed their example, perhaps as a mark of respect, or simply not to interrupt the order of things.

Very soon, she felt useless.

Yet her daily visits became a ritual that she forced herself to maintain, though as the days passed, she was less and less eager to face the atmosphere of lugubrious desolation next door. Every time she left, her heart heavy and her spirits somber, it took all the energy she had to face the evening and not let her morose mood bring Milo down. Laetitia had always had a high ideal of friendship, believing it could be truly measured only in adversity. She had set herself the task of helping Tiphaine and Sylvain get back on their feet, however long it took. As the days passed, she began to wonder if it wasn't the other way around: maybe they were dragging her down beyond hope.

David visited from time to time, although it was less frequently than his wife, given his work schedule. He saw them more often on the weekend than during the week, when he would come home late and exhausted. Laetitia soon realized that the pair of them never visited together. When David went over, she gave herself a break, vowing to return the next day. Initially she thought of it as sharing a chore, ashamed at the thought but conscious of its core truth. She took no pleasure in her visits.

Pleasure? Laetitia shivered: the thought of pleasure had just crossed her mind . . .

Because life was getting back on track for the Brunelles. And with life came wants, moments of relaxation, chatter, smiles, and sometimes even bursts of laughter, soon swallowed in ashamed embarrassment.

And above all, there was Milo.

He laid loud claim to the carefree existence he was entitled to, wanting his fair share of the spontaneity of daily life and the blithe innocence of childhood. As if to counter the gloom that hung over his home like a pall, he was buzzing with energy, almost too boisterous when he came home from school and, Laetitia soon noticed, particularly when he played outside in the yard. He would jump around, screeching, throwing his head back in laughter, sending a clear message to Tiphaine and Sylvain: *here I am.*

I am alive.

"Milo!" Laetitia reprimanded him when she first spotted what he was up to. "Get inside, now!"

"Why? It's nice outside!"

"Because I said so! Inside, now!"

Milo stalked indoors sulkily, staring at his feet, not even glancing at his mother as he stormed upstairs.

"Where are you going?" Laetitia asked, her tone softer.

"To play with Maxime."

Maxime. Milo's new stuffed animal. He was obsessed with the teddy bear, which filled his thoughts to an almost unhealthy degree. Fifty times a day, thanks to the bear, Milo said a name now ringed with the aura of the unsayable.

I'm going to play with Maxime. Where's Maxime?

I want to hug Maxime in bed.

Can I take Maxime to school? Maxime was bad today.

Maxime.

Maxime.

Maxime.

One day, at the end of her tether, Laetitia decided to address the problem directly. She stood in front of Milo and said, "We need to talk."

Milo looked at her, his expression serious. Laetitia got straight to the point. "You can't call your teddy Maxime."

"Why not?"

"Because Maxime wasn't a toy. Maxime was a little boy, like you, and he was your best friend. Maxime was Tiphaine and Sylvain's son. And above all, Maxime is dead, and every time you say his name, you remind us he's not with us anymore. And we miss him."

Milo opened his eyes wide in shock. "You want to forget Maxime?"

"No, but I want to think about him when I want to, not when you decide or just because you're playing with your teddy. Do you understand what I'm trying to say?"

Milo stood thinking for a few seconds. Then he nodded, serious and solemn. Laetitia watched his expression, worried by how he might react, and ashamed about forcing her adult concerns on his childhood play.

"I'm not saying it to make you upset or to tell you off, sweetheart. But if one day Tiphaine and Sylvain found out your new toy is called Maxime, it would make them very sad."

"OK" was Milo's only reply.

"So what would you like to call him instead? Can I help you choose another name?"

This time, Milo shook his head. Laetitia hugged him, then he scooted off to play.

The next morning, as she was making coffee, she glanced out the window. There, lying on the terrace just below Milo's bedroom window, lay the giant teddy bear.

CHAPTER 29

For Tiphaine and Sylvain, too, the days passed, with their absurd obligation to keep living, getting up, eating, putting clothes on. Maintaining a pale imitation of life against a backdrop of normality, acting a role. Pretending that after losing a child, it was possible to keep heading down the same road, eager to discover what lay beyond the next bend. To just keep going.

Blending into the crowd and never dropping the mask.

Tiphaine and Sylvain were now the parents of the little boy who died falling out his bedroom window. Everyone passing them in the street or in a store now automatically associated them with the worst ordeal a parent can face. They were the embodiment of misfortune; they bore the stamp of tragedy. Their surname was synonymous with loss, a ghoulish story people told at dinner parties, swapping cautionary tales of horrible things that happen to other people, shivering as they conclude, "How terrible, those poor parents, their lives are ruined!" And everyone would nod, thinking to themselves that their own kid might have chicken pox and that last tax return was a nightmare but their own lives were not too bad, really; worse things happen. And then someone else would come out with another, even more appalling story: quick, quick, let's hear about another misfortune that happened to someone else, something that could have happened to us if we were unlucky, although we weren't.

After their infernal descent to the borders of hell, after the unbearable pain, after the tears and the frozen inertia of the void, Tiphaine and Sylvain had to begin to think about hauling themselves back to the realm of normality. They had to force themselves to make the effort. Destroyed by their own pain, they turned inward as if to protect their own suffering: its sensation was now their main driving force. They had to try to find their footing again in a reality that was no longer their own.

"Can you pass me the milk?"

"Here you go. More coffee?"

"No, thanks."

At mealtimes, banal exchanges began to punctuate the deep-rooted silence of a tacit agreement to leave the unsayable unspoken.

"Can you pass me the milk?"

"Here you go. More coffee?"

"No, thanks."

They barely spoke to each other, just a few words here and there. What was there left to say? What, and who, was there left to talk about?

"Maxime's health insurance sent us a reminder. You did send them the death certificate, didn't you?"

" . . . "

"Tiphaine! Did you send Maxime's death certificate to the health insurance people? They want us to pay the next installment . . ."

"No, I didn't."

"You said you would do it!"

"I forgot."

"And when were you planning to get around to it?"

"If I'm not fast enough for you, feel free to do it yourself!"

Too deeply wounded to handle each other's pain, they drifted on a raft of trivial quarrels, the sort designed to close down all conversation. To shut each other up. Or just to find a moment's peace.

Sometimes the counterattack was harsher than the opening salvo.

"It's not my job," snapped Sylvain.

"Says who? Why is it up to me?"

Sylvain paused, aware that he was on the verge of a boundary he had been trying not to step over for a while. But that morning's letter about Maxime—a letter about insurance, intended to protect kids from danger, stop the worst from happening—had torn his heart to tiny shreds.

Money they were trying to make him pay, though he had lost everything.

Sylvain was in such pain that he shot back, intentionally hurtful, "Because it wasn't me who left Maxime alone in his bedroom with the window open!"

Tiphaine stiffened, her coffee cup frozen in midair. The words jostled in her brain. She must have misheard, and yet . . . lifting her horrified eyes to look Sylvain square in the face, the expression of rage twisting his features told her she had not misunderstood.

"Excuse me?"

"Don't pretend you don't understand me, Tiphaine."

"How *dare* you?"

"I do damn dare! We're going to have to talk about it one day, right? Just us two, face-to-face, eye-to-eye."

"Talk about what?"

Tiphaine's voice was lower than a murmur, barely a breath. It barely registered with Sylvain: his well of compassion had long since run dry. "About your responsibility for Maxime's death."

There. He'd said it! Better yet, to her face! The thoughts he had been holding in since the day of the accident, the conclusion that he had been chewing on relentlessly, unable to choke it down. In those early days, blaming Laetitia had been their survival strategy, a life raft they clung to in the storm to keep their heads above water. But now that the crashing waves had subsided to a gentler swell, Sylvain could not keep on lying to other people, to Tiphaine. Least of all to himself.

"We need to talk about it, Tiphaine," he added, ignoring the way her fragile presence wilted at his words. Her only response was to hunch her head into her shoulders, shrinking away from him like a snail when its eye stalks are touched.

"Because, let's face it, you *are* to blame for my son's death, aren't you?" he pursued pitilessly.

More than the accusation itself, it was the use of the possessive pronoun to exclude her as Maxime's mother that tore Tiphaine's heart a little more, if such a thing were possible.

"*Your* son?" she spat, as if the words were disease-ridden.

Sylvain clenched his teeth, studying his wife with eyes full of pain and rancor.

"*Our* son," he eventually conceded.

Tiphaine was chewing her lips, making a superhuman effort not to show her inner turmoil, trying to work out if the man across the table was an ally or an enemy. If he wished her well or was now on a mission to destroy her. For a split second, she was tempted to ask him outright.

"We can't go on like this, Tiphaine. There's just one thing I need to know."

"What?"

"If you feel responsible. For our son's death. If you realize that you are partly to blame for what happened to Maxime. Why he died."

An enemy. An adversary to fight. An opponent to defeat.

"I did nothing wrong!" she exclaimed, the words ringing hollow in her own ears.

"You left the window open, Tiphaine!" He slammed the words out, his voice chilly.

It was the coup de grace, the mortal blow that left her bleeding out, chest heaving, on the verge of death. A sob broke from her as the icy vise of guilt closed in on her. She was ready to plead guilty and step onto the scaffold. Throw down her weapons, await the verdict. End it, once and for all.

But almost against her own will, a shred of survival instinct made her fight back.

"How *dare* you!" she snapped, eyes blazing. "How *dare* you accuse me of anything! You, most of all!"

"*Me?*" Sylvain was taken aback. "Why me?"

Tiphaine gave a low, cynical snicker. "Talk about the pot calling the kettle black! Honestly, Sylvain, you really think you're in a position to preach to me about morality?"

"I'm not preaching! I just want to lay everything out on the table."

"OK, then! Let's do it!" Tiphaine's eyes were now glittering ferociously. She had found her backbone and locked eyes with Sylvain, her gaze defiant.

"What are you talking about, Tiphaine?" he asked, thrown off his stride.

"You want to talk? OK, let's talk! You know the theory that you can send anyone a letter saying, 'I know what you did.' *Anyone.* And their conscience will always accuse them of *something.*"

Sylvain stared at Tiphaine in bafflement, his brow furrowed, unclear where the conversation was leading. Pleased at the effect her words had on him, she was silent for a few seconds before declaring, slowly and dramatically, "I know what you did, Sylvain."

"What do you know?"

"Think about it."

She was laughing! Mocking him! What was she talking about? The thought whirled in Sylvain's mind without coalescing. He kept his eyes on Tiphaine, trying to find a way to throw her off. Was it a trap? Did she really know something? Was she putting her theory into practice, hoping to trick him into a confession? Or was she turning the situation around to put him in the wrong and absolve her own guilt?

He decided to sidestep her trap and shrugged indifferently.

"This is pointless," he said, feigning annoyance.

Then Tiphaine laid down her trump card.

"Stéphane Legendre," she said, her tone implacable. "The fake prescription. The court case. My life destroyed for a mistake I never made . . ."

CHAPTER 30

Sylvain was dumbstruck. A haze of hypotheses and conjectures milled through his mind as he tried to work out how Tiphaine could know. Stupefaction stopped him putting his thoughts in order and the pressing need for an explanation paralyzed him even more.

She knew! Since when? And above all, *how*?

Suddenly, his blood froze. David! David must have told her. No one else knew, did they?

"That *bastard*!" he hissed violently, barely keeping control.

"With friends like that, who needs enemies, right?" Tiphaine murmured, her voice a whisper.

"When did he tell you?"

"Just before he died."

For the second time in under two minutes, Sylvain felt the blood drain from his body. He stared at Tiphaine in bewilderment, sure his heart was about to stop.

"D . . . David?" he stammered. "David is *dead*?"

Tiphaine's expression changed. "What are you on about?"

"You just said . . ."

"I wasn't talking about David!"

They stared at each other for long seconds in total incomprehension. Tiphaine had no idea why Sylvain had brought David into the conversation and Sylvain had no idea who she was talking about.

"*David* knew?" she roared suddenly as the source of the misunderstanding hit her. "You mean you told David everything and I had no idea?"

"I . . ."

Tiphaine's face crumpled into a twisted mask of bitterness and hatred. "You *bastard*!" she spat. "You've been lying to me since we met, you betrayed me, and then you went and told David everything! Oh, you must have had fun laughing at me behind my back!"

"No!" cried Sylvain, aghast at how completely the situation had slipped from his control. "Absolutely not! I . . . David . . ."

"What about Laetitia? I bet she knows, too! I'm the only idiot still in the dark, am I? You must all think I'm so damn stupid!"

Sylvain numbly held out a hand to Tiphaine, but she slapped it away. "Don't you *dare* touch me! You utter bastard! How could you! All these years . . ."

A sob rising in her throat forced her to stop. She hid her face in her hands. Sylvain stood in front of her, arms dangling limply by his sides, mortified by the turn of events. Tiphaine had started the conversation as the guilty party, but *she* was now the innocent victim, boldly accusing *him* of the most terrible act. He was completely lost. If David hadn't shared his secret, who had? Definitely not Laetitia, since Tiphaine didn't know she didn't know. Who, then? No one else knew. Except . . .

Then it struck him. The only person who could have revealed his secret was none other than Stéphane Legendre himself, the day he came to visit. Clearly, Tiphaine must have been home that afternoon when his former best friend rang the doorbell. She must have opened the door and let him in. Gradually, he imagined the scene, the pictures forming sinuous, whirling arabesques in his shocked mind. Stéphane Legendre ringing the bell. Tiphaine opening the door, asking who he is and what he wants. Stéphane asking if this is Sylvain's house. Tiphaine saying her husband is out, but Stéphane is welcome to come back later that evening if he likes. Stéphane saying thank you, no need, he has come to see her, not him . . . Why would he do something like that? Why, after all those years, would he have gone to all the effort of tracking them down, then travel all the way from Paris, just to spill the secret to Tiphaine? Stéphane Legendre had only ever been interested in one person. Himself.

Sylvain was completely lost.

"*Stéphane* told you?" he stammered out, trying to bring order to his thoughts.

"Well, *you* didn't!" she seethed.

He stared at her, struggling to try and understand what must have happened. Tiphaine was now fully in control of her emotions.

"What did he tell you?"

"The truth."

"Tell me what he told you, Tiphaine!"

"Everything! He told me everything! His own professional

misconduct, your involvement to keep him out of trouble, swapping the prescriptions . . . how we met . . ."

"But *why*? Why now, after all these years?"

She shrugged as if it were a meaningless detail. "He was sick. He knew he was going to die. He wanted to salve his conscience . . ."

"Bullshit!"

They sat silent for a moment, each of them tangled in the shadowy web of their own resentment, torn between anger and torment, gauging to what extent their own fault stripped them of the right to demand justice. Sylvain felt atomized, exploded into fragments filling the room. Words failed him as, wild-eyed, he tried weakly to pull himself together. Tiphaine, on the other hand, was using her pain as justification for her demands. Eventually, she murmured in a broken voice, "I paid a heavy price for the loss of a baby, when I hadn't done anything wrong!"

"What baby are you talking about?"

"The one the woman was carrying. The one your friend killed with his prescription."

"That's got nothing to do with us!"

"Of course it does! You always end up paying the price, Sylvain! Stéphane Legendre's guilt ate away at him until it turned into cancer and killed him."

Sylvain frowned, not sure he understood her insinuations. Then, suddenly, the concepts of fault and punishment echoed through him like an accusation. He opened his eyes wide in disgust.

"If you're trying to blame me for Maxime's death on the grounds that I had to pay one way or another . . ."

"I'm not trying to do anything of the sort, Sylvain," she snapped, clearly irritated. "Don't act like I'm an idiot."

"What, then?"

Tiphaine was silent for a moment before she explained. "You've already destroyed my life once. There won't be a second time."

"Your life? What life?" Sylvain forced a bitter laugh. "We don't *have* a life anymore, Tiphaine. All we have left is time, stretching out in front of us. Time for suffering."

"You've already rebuilt my life once."

"What exactly is it you want?"

"I want everything to go back to the way it was before."

Sylvain stared wildly at her. The mere thought of the past, of a time of happiness lost forever, broke his heart. As if a blade of ice had pierced it, causing unbearable pain. He burst into tears. "That can never happen," he moaned, his voice broken.

Tiphaine stood up, walked around the table, and came to stand by his side. Then, almost maternally, she pulled him into her arms and began rocking him like a child. Sylvain clung to her like a drowning man.

"It *can* happen, sweetheart," she murmured softly. "We just have to start over."

Blinking back the tears, he looked up at her, his eyes filled with distress and confusion. "Start over?"

"I want another child."

The shock dried his tears. They gazed long and deep into each other's eyes. For the first time since the tragedy, they saw in each other the spark of love that had died with Maxime.

"What about you?" she asked, her words full of hope.

He could not speak for the lump in his throat, so he simply nodded.

Now it was Tiphaine's turn to cry.

CHAPTER 31

Tiphaine and Sylvain had recently returned to work, to Laetitia's great relief: their long period of apathy was beginning to make her nervous. She was still visiting them, or rather visiting Tiphaine, since Sylvain was spending most of his time at the architecture firm to make up for lost time. At least, that was the official reason.

"He's hiding behind his work," Tiphaine complained over a cup of coffee. "It feels like he leaves earlier every morning and gets back later every night."

"It's his way of dealing with Maxime not being here," Laetitia suggested gently.

"Or maybe he's just avoiding me."

Laetitia took in Tiphaine's comment. She knew that the loss of a child often spelled the death knell for a relationship, each parent embodying the tragedy in the other's eyes. "What makes you say that?" she asked carefully.

Tiphaine shrugged nonchalantly, as if it were a throwaway comment. But the tears that sprang from her eyes betrayed her real feelings. "He blames me for Maxime's death."

Laetitia bit her lower lip. She wouldn't go so far as to blame Tiphaine altogether, but there was no denying she had been criminally negligent to leave a six-year-old child alone in a room with an open window. Even if he was asleep. The memory of Tiphaine criticizing her for leaving the children alone upstairs when they scribbled on each other's face with markers came unbidden to her mind.

Laetitia kept her thoughts to herself.

"If he really thought you were to blame for Maxime's death, he would already have left you," she pointed out with as much confidence as she could muster. "You know what I think? You blame yourself for the . . . accident."

A stab of pain flashed in Tiphaine's eyes, a glimpse of the torture she had been enduring for weeks.

"Of course I blame myself!" she snapped, her voice broken by a sob. "I *am* to blame, aren't I? I left my little boy all alone in his bedroom with the window wide open! What mother worthy of the name would have made such a stupid mistake?"

"It was an accident!" Laetitia immediately replied, choked with emotion at her friend's confession. "He was asleep. How were you to know he would wake up as soon as you left? You are a good mother, Tiphaine. You always were . . ."

She fell silent, trying to think of other arguments to console Tiphaine.

"I would probably have done the exact same thing," she lied, with an assurance she was far from feeling.

Neither spoke for a while, conscious they were teetering at the top of a slippery slope. Laetitia gently tried to steer the conversation in another direction. "And how is your job going?"

"Who gives a shit about work?" Tiphaine said dismissively.

"It's just a way of filling the days. And it's better than sitting around the house on my own."

The unexpected answer left Laetitia at a loss. She said nothing.

This time, Tiphaine broke the silence. "Laetitia . . ." She hesitated, her voice full of embarrassment. "I'd like . . . I'd like to see Milo."

The unexpected request left Laetitia lost for words.

"I'm still his godmother," Tiphaine added, as if to justify her request.

"Of course," mumbled Laetitia. It was not clear if she was confirming Tiphaine was still his godmother or if she was agreeing to let her see him.

An unspoken fear twisted a knot in her stomach, as if the idea of entrusting her child to Tiphaine filled her with terror. Had losing her son made Tiphaine untrustworthy? Following on the heels of her confession of guilt, the request had the undertone of a hidden threat. And had Tiphaine cunningly tricked her into acknowledging she was still a great mom?

"You are a good mother, Tiphaine. You always were . . ."

Her instinctive reaction to Tiphaine's question was a hard no. Yet after a moment's thought, that seemed unfair: did a few minutes' negligence really undo six years of unwavering maternal devotion? Of course not. She had never hesitated to leave Milo with Tiphaine before. So why the barely disguised anxiety now?

Disconcerted by her inner alarm bells ringing at full blast, Laetitia simply stared at her friend, who was clearly waiting for her to say something.

"See Milo? Yes . . . of course, why not?" Laetitia sounded unenthusiastic, even to her own ears. Tiphaine could not fail to feel it too.

"You don't like the idea, do you?" murmured Tiphaine, her distress clear from her tone.

"Of course I do!" Laetitia exclaimed, forcing herself to sound convincing. "It's just that . . ." She trailed off, sounding faker than ever. Realizing that she was digging herself into a hole, she cast around for an excuse or argument that would make Tiphaine see the situation from her point of view.

"Milo's not doing great right now. Maxime's death has affected him deeply, as I'm sure you can imagine, and . . . well, you might as well know, we're taking him to see a child psychiatrist next week."

Finding Milo's teddy bear on the terrace under his window had freaked David and Laetitia out. They talked it over and decided to take their son to see a specialist to help him get over the ordeal. He was clearly refusing to face up to it. Laetitia had made inquiries with his teacher, who had put her in touch with Justine Philippot. She came highly recommended.

Tiphaine didn't take the hint. "He needs to see us. Have you noticed the noise he makes whenever he's in the yard? I'm sure he's trying to catch our attention. It's his way of reaching out to us."

"That's true," conceded Laetitia.

"Let me have him over on Saturday afternoon. I'm sure he'd like that just as much as I would."

Laetitia nodded pensively, torn between her irrational sense of panic and the lack of a rational argument for turning

Tiphaine down. Subconsciously, she, too, thought of Tiphaine as being shrouded in unhappiness, and the thought of leaving her little boy to face this distress twisted a knot deep in her gut.

Seeing Laetitia was still reluctant, Tiphaine played her trump card. "Ask him!" she suggested. "Let him decide."

It was clear to see she was desperate, a hair's breadth from falling to her knees and begging. Laetitia found herself in the strange position of judge, jury, and executioner.

"OK," she said. Deep down inside, she knew Tiphaine had painted her into a corner.

CHAPTER 32

Milo accepted Tiphaine's invitation with an enthusiasm that surprised his mother, making her rethink her own attitude. What if what he wanted most of all was to see Tiphaine and Sylvain again, or at least not feel rejected by them? He must have felt as if they were shunning him, between the accident and the funeral. It occurred to Laetitia that whenever she had tried talking to him about Maxime's death, she had focused on the tragedy without going into its hideous consequences— the way his godmother had rejected her and hurled monstrous accusations. Even though Milo had never witnessed any of the clashes between his parents and Maxime's, he must have sensed their disquiet without being able to put a name to it. That must have been worse than anything. Children are so sensitive.

David thought it was a great idea when he saw how happy Milo was at the suggestion. When Laetitia told him she had nearly refused, he was taken aback.

"What do you think will happen to him?" he asked. "He's been visiting Tiphaine and Sylvain since he was born."

"I know," she admitted. "I was probably worried about him having to deal with their grief."

"Well, what about it? Parents who have just lost their child will be grieving, won't they? That's to be expected. It would be absurd to try to insulate him from it completely. Tiphaine and Sylvain are like his second mom and dad. If you stop him seeing them, he really will have lost everything."

"That's a fair point . . ."

Reassured by David's point of view, Laetitia felt her trust in Tiphaine return. With a certain sense of serenity and the feeling of doing the right thing, she took him next door the following Saturday after lunch.

Tiphaine welcomed Milo with a surge of emotion she did not try to hide. She threw open the door, knelt down, and hugged him long and close. "I'm so pleased to see you," she said. "I've missed you, you know."

"Me too, Auntiphaine."

"Wanna get an ice cream at the park?" she suggested.

Milo nodded vigorously with a loud "Yeah!"

"One ice cream, coming right up!" Tiphaine laughed. She turned to Laetitia. "OK if I bring him back around five?"

Laetitia nodded. She hadn't seen Tiphaine laugh since Maxime's death, and she was pleased. As she turned to leave, Tiphaine threw her arms around her. "Thanks, Laetitia."

"What for?"

"Letting me look after him," Tiphaine replied, tilting her head in Milo's direction. Laetitia shrugged as if to say there was no need for thanks, then went back home.

She kept herself busy all afternoon, finishing all the little jobs she couldn't get around to when Milo was in the way. She cleaned his bedroom from top to bottom, then caught up with some files she hadn't managed to finish at work. David was out in the taxi—he picked up the occasional weekend shift—so she was home alone. She took a well-earned break at around four, sitting out on the terrace with coffee and a magazine.

It was warm and summery. The air was still, and the calm house and yard gave Laetitia a sense of well-being that brought a sigh of contentment to her lips. Finding herself alone and relaxed, she treated herself to a cigarette.

"Are you smoking, Mom?"

Milo's voice broke into her reverie. Laetitia started in surprise, unable to tell where the sound was coming from. She had thought she was alone.

"Here, Mom!" Milo called out happily.

"Where?" she asked, a note of anxiety in her voice as she glanced around.

"Up here!"

Laetitia looked up and saw to her horror that Milo was leaning out Maxime's bedroom window, clutching a bottle of bubble mix. The bubbles drifted across the hedge. She screamed. "Milo! Get down right now! Get back in the bedroom!"

He ignored her, merrily waving from the window.

She thought she would go mad. Instinctively, she grabbed her chair, dragged it over to the hedge, climbed on it, and threw herself over. The hedge was nearly six feet tall, so she had to straddle the top and jump. She leaped down without a second's hesitation. Two seconds later, she was in next door's yard, her legs scratched and bruised. She dashed to the terrace under Maxime's window, ignoring the pain.

"Get back inside! Now!" she screeched at Milo.

"But I'm blowing bubbles, Mom!"

"What's got into you, Laetitia?" Tiphaine asked, appearing at the window.

Panting for breath, Laetitia gave her friend a frenzied stare. "Are you completely insane?" she roared in a voice full of rebuke.

"There's nothing to worry about," Tiphaine said defensively. "He's just blowing bubbles. I'm right next to him. He's perfectly safe."

Laetitia was speechless. She felt personally assaulted by Tiphaine's crazy recklessness, so soon after Maxime's accident—same place, same circumstances, almost the same time of day . . . so many parallels were surely no coincidence. Laetitia's fear turned to rage. "What is your problem? After what happened, how can you even *think* of letting Milo near a window!"

Tiphaine looked offended, unable to mask her outrage at Laetitia's thinly veiled accusations. "I'm right next to him!" she repeated, humiliation written all over her face. "I've been with him all afternoon, in the park and at home. Who do you take me for?"

Milo heard every word of their angry exchange. Frowning with worry, he looked from one to the other without a word. Seeing his expression, Laetitia softened her tone. She did not want him to be scared.

"Sorry . . . I was scared. I thought I was going to live through the same nightmare as that afternoon." The words sounded defensive. Tiphaine studied her face, as if reluctant to accept her apology. From her vantage point by the window, she looked down at Laetitia, who was forced to raise her head to talk to them. Tiphaine's face relaxed, though she still looked concerned. She gave a small, sad smile. "I'm sorry, Laetitia. It's my fault. I should have been more considerate."

The two women remained silent for a few moments, their mutual apologies hanging in the air. Milo seemed relieved.

"What . . . what are you doing in Maxime's bedroom?" Laetitia eventually asked.

"I told Milo he could choose a few toys if he wants."

The exceptionally generous gesture caught Laetitia off guard. "Are you sure?"

"Sylvain and I have been thinking a lot. We don't want to be like those parents who keep their dead child's bedroom untouched for years on end, like a shrine. Sylvain agrees with me. We want to fight for life. We want other little boys to enjoy Maxime's toys. The sooner, the better. I'm sure it's what he would have wanted. We've already put away the things we want to keep. Life goes on, Laetitia. I have to tell myself that. Milo can have what he wants, he gets first pick. We're choosing what he would like most. Would you like to come up and join us?"

Laetitia couldn't believe it. Staggered by Tiphaine's remarkable, unforeseen reaction, she could not help but admire her strength, so soon after her son's death. "I'm on my way!" she called, smiling at her friend in admiration.

She joined them in Maxime's room. As she passed the door, she suppressed a shiver of fear at seeing the room again. She pushed the vision of the little boy broken on the terrace below from her mind, hugging Milo happily and—she couldn't deny it—with a slight sense of relief.

They spent the rest of the afternoon together. Milo chose a remote-control crane he and Maxime had often played with, a truck, two jigsaw puzzles, a box of Lego, a few books, and a construction set. They went downstairs, where Milo played with his new toys while Tiphaine and Laetitia settled down to their favorite pastime: chatting over a cup of coffee.

Milo and Laetitia went home at about six.

Later that evening, Tiphaine told Sylvain about spending the afternoon with Milo, the episode at the window, and Laetitia's terror.

"So what do you make of it?" Sylvain asked when she finished talking.

"When it came to saving her own son, she was in our yard in under five seconds," Tiphaine replied, tears spilling from her eyes.

CHILD MEDICAL RECORD

AGE 6–7

Your child's adult teeth should be coming in. How many teeth has your child lost?

> Three: the top two incisors (the adult teeth are growing in) and the lower canine. M. has a wonderful gap-toothed smile!

Your child needs a good breakfast to set them up for the day. What does your child eat in the mornings?

> Chocolate cereal (usually one bowl), sometimes a slice of toast and honey. M. has a healthy appetite and eats well at every meal.

DOCTOR'S NOTES:

> Weight: 44 lb. Height: 3 ft. 11 in.

CHAPTER 33

Justine Philippot was as generous as her curves. She bore her fifty-three years proudly in a dress patterned with sprigs of spring flowers. Her hair was graying naturally and her face showed no trace of makeup. Her temperament matched her outward appearance—warm and cheerful. She prided herself on being forthright and always speaking her mind. That did not mean she voiced every passing thought. Justine Philippot knew from experience that some truths were best left unsaid, and in her profession, those truths could take years to surface.

She ushered Milo and his parents into her office, a huge, brightly sunlit room split into three areas. An imposing desk dominated the far wall, while in the right-hand side of the room a couch and armchair were positioned facing each other. A low table stood in between, with a box of tissues in easy reach. To the left was a rug marking a small play area with boxes of toys for Justine's young patients.

"So, what brings you to see me?" she asked as David and Laetitia settled into the two chairs at her desk. Laetitia gave her a brief version of events: Maxime's tragic death, his mother's crazed accusations, their confrontation and reconciliation. She then moved onto Milo's reaction, his apparent lack of grief, what happened with Bunnikins, the scene at Maxime's funeral, buying the new teddy bear, Milo's choice of name, the teddy bear falling from his window.

As she was talking, Milo wandered over to the toys and began playing on the rug.

When Laetitia finished, Justine's first question was "What was the relationship like between Maxime and Milo?"

It was David who replied. "They were best friends. They were the same age and practically grew up together. They were like brothers."

"Was there ever any rivalry between them?"

David and Laetitia both shook their heads.

"They argued every now and then, of course, but I never felt they were in competition for anything," Laetitia added.

"And what about you two? How did you feel about Maxime?"

"We loved him," Laetitia said as if it were obvious.

"Like a son?"

"No, of course not . . . more like a nephew, I'd say."

Justine Philippot probed gently, fleshing out the picture of their lives before Maxime's death. She explored their emotional response to Tiphaine's violent accusations and the close friendship between the two couples, mirrored in the relationship between the two boys.

"It sounds to me like Maxime was Milo's ideal brother. They each had their own house and parents, neither crowded into the other's emotional space but was always around whenever they wanted. They played together every day but when it was over they went home to their own parents. No jealousy, no unwelcome presence, no competition."

David and Laetitia nodded.

"A bit like a teddy that you can play with whenever you like but then put away in a drawer when you've had enough," Justine added.

The comparison shed fresh light on Milo's behavior for Laetitia, and she could not hold back a smile.

"Yes, you could put it like that, I suppose."

"Except Maxime wasn't Milo's teddy, was he?" David pointed out.

"No, but clearly, Milo's teddy has taken Maxime's place."

"Is . . . is that a good thing?" Laetitia asked hesitantly.

Justine thought for a few seconds. "It's not concerning. Not at this stage of the mourning process, anyway. Children invent imaginary friends to meet a need, and Milo is meeting the need left by Maxime's death with the means at his disposal."

"So why did he throw the bear out the window?"

"Because you asked him to deny his bear's identity. It was his way of giving him his identity back, by making the same thing happen to him as to Maxime."

Laetitia shivered. "So I shouldn't have told him to change the bear's name?"

"In all honesty? No, you shouldn't have. But what's done is done and no real harm has come to Milo. Your son is very resilient, he's already shown that."

Laetitia nodded pensively, her face drawn with guilt.

David sat up straight on his chair, leaned toward Justine, and asked in a low voice, "Why has he never cried about Maxime?"

He clearly did not want to be overheard by Milo, who seemed to be playing happily without paying attention to the grown-ups.

"Let me set you straight there, Mr. Brunelle. Your son *has* cried for his friend," Justine replied, without lowering her voice. "But when he does, he attributes it to other causes, and it comes out as changes in behavior. The important take-home message for you today is that Milo's reactions and behavior are his way of laying claim to a carefree childhood. By going on as if nothing had happened, he is simply showing you he intends to devote his time and energy to being a normal little boy. But that doesn't mean he is refusing to face up to his friend's death."

"So you think there's no need to worry?" Laetitia asked.

"That's not what I said," Justine responded. "What I mean is, Milo is grieving in his own way, though it might not be obvious to you. That's why you came to see me, isn't it?"

David and Laetitia both nodded again.

"But it would be a mistake to think that just because he has come up with his own instinctive coping mechanism, he doesn't need any help. What I would recommend, if you're on board, is a short course of therapy to help all three of you through this tough patch."

"Do you think we really need it?" asked Laetitia. She didn't like the thought of family therapy, but wasn't outright rejecting it.

"The close bond the three of you share with your neighbors

is like a family relationship. You said it: Maxime and Milo were like brothers and you loved Maxime like a nephew. Maxime's death will certainly have quite an impact on Milo's life. You, his parents, can see that when you fell out with your friends after the tragedy, it was because they are *not* family. You can readjust your priorities accordingly. Milo may not be able to. In his mind, and above in all in his heart, he has lost his brother."

David and Laetitia looked at each other, but said nothing.

"I don't need a yes or no right away," Justine continued. "Talk about it at home, then get back to me."

The consultation was over. David and Laetitia paid and left with Milo. They walked along silently for a few minutes, mulling over Justine's words.

"She never even talked to him," Laetitia suddenly murmured, gesturing to Milo as he raced ahead of them to the car.

"Sixty euros!" David grumbled. "A whole course of therapy will cost a fortune."

"Especially as I can't really see the point for Milo," Laetitia agreed, shrugging. They walked on, both lost in their own thoughts.

"Can I call my teddy Maxime now?" Milo suddenly asked, turning triumphantly to his parents.

CHAPTER 34

That year, Milo's birthday fell on a Saturday. David and Laetitia had planned an afternoon party for his classmates and their parents. The house and yard were crowded with excited children. Spring seemed to have settled in for the long run. Laetitia had been busy baking desserts, including a fruit tart, an almond loaf, and a huge chocolate cake that were all wolfed down in seconds. David oversaw the party games: musical chairs won—perhaps not coincidentally—by Milo, charades that the adults joined in, and a treasure hunt that delighted the youngest children. The mood was joyful, and cries of joy and shouts of laughter filled the air as the children ran wild.

Ernest was one of the guests. Milo was growing more and more attached to the old man as he grew up, enjoying his company and begging for thrilling stories about catching bad guys. Ernest was by no means the ideal godfather. He rarely visited, and when he did, he was usually awkward, impatient, irascible, and thoughtless. His presents were often completely inappropriate. The year before, he had bought Milo two tickets to a wrestling match in Paris. Laetitia, who was not a wrestling fan, banned Milo from what she called the "violent, obscene display." But though Ernest had little in common with the rest of the guests, he never missed one of Milo's birthday parties. He never stayed for very long. He'd make an entrance that stood out among the hordes of overexcited children milling around, and then head off quietly as soon as Milo had blown out the candles on the cake.

The year Milo turned seven was no exception.

Tiphaine and Sylvain were invited, of course. Laetitia made it clear she would understand perfectly if they preferred not to come, if the memory of the previous years was too painful. They had promised to stop by, at least—Tiphaine did not want to miss her godson's seventh birthday. Seven: the age of reason. At least, that was what she said. Laetitia waited a while before bringing out the cake decorated with seven candles, but when she saw it was past four o'clock and Tiphaine and Sylvain still hadn't put in an appearance, she decided to check in next door.

No one answered when she rang the bell, which only half surprised her. She thought they must be in. Their car was parked just down the road. They were at home, she was sure of it. For reasons that were only all too easy to guess, they had not found the strength to come and join in the fun.

That day, of all days, Maxime's absence stared them in the face.

Milo was seven. Maxime would never be seven.

Laetitia worried for a moment about what would have been Maxime's own birthday, in a little under three months' time. She hesitated for a moment, then decided to leave them alone and return to her guests. Turning around, she went back home. Ernest had already shown some signs of impatience, eager to leave the noise and chaos of the party. Time to cut the cake.

Tiphaine and Sylvain could hear the sounds of the party in the kitchen, through the tightly closed windows and terrace doors. The joyful hubbub of children shouting, laughing, and running around echoed through the heavy silence that hung over the house. Tiphaine stood by the counter, lost in her recipe, spooning ingredients into her blender. When the doorbell rang, she froze and held her breath.

It must be Laetitia. Wondering where they were, so she could cut the cake.

She wavered for a second. Should she open the door and explain, apologize, back out of the party? The cheerful atmosphere, the laughter, the smiles, the colors, the joy . . . it was all too much. More than she could take. If she went, she would spend every second fending off the grief that threatened to engulf her, making a superhuman effort to pin the ghost of a smile to her face as she fought back tears in the midst of the happy crowd. Better to stay safely at home, away from the sly sidelong glances and whispered gossip. Away from the sense of burning shame.

Away from joy.

Tiphaine stood frozen, chilled to the bone, torn, terrified the bell would ring again.

Silence reigned.

A minute or two later, she glimpsed movement on the other side of the front door and realized Laetitia was going back home to keep celebrating her little boy's seventh birthday.

Tiphaine slowly returned to her task, gripping her wooden spoon like a life raft.

Next door, Milo's guests were singing their hearts out. Milo blew out the candles and everyone clapped. The kids were having a wonderful time.

Like every year, Ernest came over to Laetitia while the children were eating their cake to whisper a discreet goodbye.

"Already!" she teased him. "We've only just cut the cake!"

"Milo can have my slice." He smiled.

"No way! Far too much sugar. He'll be sick." She wiped her hands on a dishtowel and turned her attention to him fully. "How are you doing, Ernest?"

"Can't complain."

"How's the leg?"

"Oh, we have a deal, you know how it is. I don't bug it, it doesn't bug me. Before, I could hardly *stand* it but I think it's going *tibia* OK!"

He hooted with laughter. Laetitia smiled fondly, shaking her head indulgently. Ernest loved bad puns and liked nothing better than laughing at his own jokes. He eventually stopped chuckling and turned serious again. "No, the big problem right now is my back."

"Really?"

"I'm getting old, you know!"

"Don't be silly."

"No, seriously! I have to do physical therapy and I'm supposed to go swimming twice a week. Ugh, no way. The water in public pools is swarming with gross little creatures."

"You know, they're much cleaner than they used to be . . ."

"I mean kids . . ."

This time it was Laetitia's turn to laugh. She took his arm and walked with him to the front door. "Why don't you come for dinner one of these days?"

"I'd like that. Only if you cook your famous ham hock and lentils."

"Would you like that?"

He nodded eagerly, his mouth watering at the thought.

"Ham hock and lentils it is, then," promised Laetitia. She planted a warm kiss on his cheek and closed the door behind the old man.

CHAPTER 35

The last guests left at around seven. It took David a good half hour to clean up while Laetitia got Milo ready for bed. His last job was taking the trash can out to the sidewalk.

A crowd at the end of the street immediately caught his eye. A police car and ambulance were parked, their lights flashing. David went over to see what was going on, intrigued by the unexpected sight in a peaceful neighborhood where, frankly, nothing much ever happened. The throng of onlookers was too closely packed for him to get a good look.

"What's going on?" he asked the man next to him.

"Heart attack. That's all I know."

David craned his neck to see, but all he could make out was a corner of a stretcher carrying a body. He was about to turn back and head home when a group of three people stepped away, leaving a gap in the crowd. David shuffled forward automatically.

The body lay under a white sheet. Clearly, help had come too late. The paramedics were about to hoist the stretcher into the ambulance.

As they lifted the stretcher, it tipped slightly to one side and an arm flopped out. The ambulance's swirling blue light bounced off the cars, the houses, and the onlookers' faces, creating a dramatic sense of foreboding.

David, who had been watching the scene with vague interest, found his gaze magnetically drawn by the arm that swung limply as the paramedics made for the ambulance.

"Wait!" he yelled frantically, pushing his way through the crowd.

Not waiting for permission, he grabbed the wrist and took a close look at the dead man's watch. His breathing quickened.

Shocked and incredulous, he looked up at the paramedics, frowning, his eyes filled with fear and anguish and his throat constricted.

"I think I know him. Let me see his face," he pleaded, his voice blank.

The two stretcher bearers conferred briefly, then nodded. His mouth dry, David reached for the sheet covering the man's head. The suspense was short-lived. He pulled back the fabric and saw Ernest, his skin sallow and his features frozen in a snarl of agony.

CHAPTER 36

Despite his distress and confusion, David immediately saw a contradiction in the details shared by the paramedics as they took Ernest's body away. The symptoms, time of death, and account of events made no sense to him.

A neighbor returning home after walking his dog had passed Ernest staggering around in the street shortly before seven. The neighbor had thought at the time that the old man had had too much to drink.

"He was weaving along like he'd been on a bender," he kept explaining to anyone who would listen. "He was stumbling around, barely able to stand upright. Then he leaned against the wall and began throwing up. I figured it was the booze! None of my business, I thought, so I just walked on by."

Ten minutes later, two more neighbors were driving home. The father, Mr. Mansion, parked near Ernest. By then, the old man was on his knees, bent double, clutching his chest, his features twisted in agony. Mr. Mansion rushed out of the car to ask if he needed help, while his wife dialed the emergency services.

The ambulance arrived within a couple of minutes. The

crew immediately diagnosed a heart attack and tried to save Ernest. In vain. The old man died shortly after, at 7:36 p.m.

Befuddled with grief, David took in the details but could not make sense of them.

"Did you know this man?" a policeman asked.

David nodded blankly. "He was my son's godfather . . ."

"Can you come with us to ID him?"

"I need to let my wife know first."

Another policeman joined them, whispering a message in the first policeman's ear. He nodded. "I'll take your details down and you can come along to the station and give us a statement tomorrow."

David gave him all the information he needed, then asked which hospital Ernest had been taken to. The ambulance had gone and there was nothing left to see. The crowd was breaking up as people wandered home, alone or in small groups, gossiping about the scene they had just witnessed.

Thoroughly despondent, David went home.

As he walked the few yards back to his house, he was assailed by a host of thoughts and questions. How could he break the news of Ernest's tragic death to Laetitia? Should they tell Milo, who barely seemed to be getting over the loss of Maxime? How would the little boy take another death in his close circle? David was working hard to keep calm. He had to come to a decision right away: he had already been out far longer than it took to put the trash can by the street. Laetitia would be wondering what was up. Yet he was sure of one thing: Milo did not need to hear about Ernest. Not yet. Not tonight. Let the boy enjoy his birthday to the very end.

As he reached the house, he saw Laetitia come out looking for him.

"Where were you?" she asked, more curious than worried.

"Everything's fine," he replied, trying to keep his expression neutral.

"What's going on over there?" Laetitia continued, spotting the flashing blue lights and people standing around at the end of the street.

"Nothing. Some poor schmuck had too much to drink. Come on, let's get inside."

David decided to wait until Milo was in bed before telling Laetitia. The following hour, as he tried to act normal while getting Milo ready for bed, felt as if it would never end.

Once she'd gotten over the initial shock, Laetitia immediately identified the incongruous detail.

"I don't understand," she sobbed, looking at David with devastation in her eyes. "He left here at half past four. How come he was still on our street at seven? What was he doing for two and a half hours?"

"I have no idea," David murmured.

"Something must have happened to him in the meantime. I don't understand . . ."

David shook his head, baffled. "I have to go to the police station tomorrow to make a statement. I'm sure they'll be able to tell us more."

It was a depressing end to the day. They looked at the mystery from all angles, but neither could come up with a plausible explanation for the gap in Ernest's afternoon.

Laetitia went over her last exchange with the old man, a lump in her throat. "It doesn't make any sense!" she exclaimed suddenly.

"I know . . ."

"No, I don't mean the time . . . he had a heart attack, right?"

"That's what the ambulance crew said."

Laetitia seemed frantic all of a sudden. "When I walked him to the door this afternoon, he told me his back was giving him trouble."

"And?"

"At Ernest's age, when you have a heart attack, it's because you have a weak heart, right?"

"I guess so."

"Can you have a fatal heart attack without any warning signs?"

"What are you getting at?"

Laetitia tutted impatiently. "If Ernest had heart problems, he would have mentioned it, wouldn't he? But he didn't. He just told me about his back."

"What are you trying to say?"

"Nothing. I was just thinking that Ernest didn't have a weak heart."

David sighed. He didn't like the turn the conversation was taking.

"Will you tell the police tomorrow?" Laetitia insisted.

"Tell them what?"

"That as far as we know, Ernest didn't have heart problems. And there's a two-and-a-half-hour gap in his afternoon."

Lost in painful thoughts, David said nothing for several long seconds. The more he thought about it, the more mysterious Ernest's death seemed. What sordid mess had his old friend got himself tangled up in? David knew that though Ernest had been retired for about five years, he still knew plenty of shady people.

He also thought that his own situation as an ex-junkie with time inside would **not play** in his favor. He sure as hell did not want to get involved in all that again.

"David!" Laetitia interrupted his train of thought. "You will tell them, right?"

For a brief instant, he was tempted to share his thoughts with her. But he held back.

"If you insist . . . ," he said, giving in with a sigh.

CHAPTER 37

David soon realized that the police did not consider Ernest's death to be suspicious. There were no signs of physical assault and the forensic pathologist agreed it was a heart attack that killed him. He was sixty-five; these things happened.

Having spent too much time on the wrong side of the table in police stations, David was on guard throughout the interview. He said as little as he could while answering their questions about his relationship with the dead man, what had brought Ernest to their neighborhood—a long way from his own—and what he had been doing in the hours leading up to his death.

David made it clear that Ernest had left the birthday party at around half-past four.

He spoke in monosyllables, nodding or shaking his head. The false sense of calm at the police station made him feel uneasy, and he could not help but remember the times when his conscience was not as clear as it was now. He forced himself to look like he was in control, confident in his information and his reactions. He was no longer a young guy up to his neck in petty crime. He had done nothing wrong.

"Thanks, that will be all," the policeman eventually said,

finishing his notes. David remained impassive, thinking back to longer, less polite interrogations. Surprised by the witness's lack of reaction, the policeman looked up at him.

"That will be all," he repeated, his gaze insistent.

"So . . . no investigation?"

"That's not for me to decide," the policeman replied. It was clear that for him, the case was closed.

For a brief instant, relief washed over David. His painful past was a reminder that the less he came into contact with the police, the better. He nodded again and gathered his things, glad to leave a place that put him on edge. Then he remembered Laetitia's doubts and his promise that he would voice their suspicions. Unable to hide his reluctance, he looked once more at the policeman behind his desk, who now had a look of exasperation on his face. David stared at him, reading in his eyes how much the man disliked him. The naked hostility unsettled him and he immediately felt the old, familiar sense of oppression. He could not wait to get out of there.

Did he need to belabor the point? After all, the police usually took cases seriously, as he knew from personal experience. Ernest's wry smile flashed before his eyes, and for a second, he missed his old friend bitterly. What had happened? Was Laetitia right to think there was something suspicious about his death? David told himself that he had told the police everything they needed to know to arrive at the same conclusions as his wife. What more could he do? His years of petty crime had deepened his natural reserve. The less he drew attention to himself, the better. He didn't need the hassle.

The advice Ernest had hammered into him after his years in prison rang in his ears. Mind your own business. Keep to yourself.

"Is there anything else?" asked the policeman. It was clear from his tone that the interview was over.

Brought back to earth with a jolt, David tensed up. No, that was all. All he wanted was to get out of there and go home.

He shook his head, stood up, and strode out without looking back.

CHAPTER 38

Ernest's death cast a further dark pall over David's and Laetitia's lives. Like a curse. The death of two people in their inner circle in under three months made them suspicious of a fate they no longer felt was their own. The aura of mystery hanging over Ernest's death added to their anxiety.

They had to break the news to Milo, framing it as a natural part of life. Old people die, that's just the way it is.

Milo was inconsolable.

Unlike Maxime's death, Milo wept long and hard when Ernest died. Laetitia was almost relieved, much preferring to see her son express his sadness rather than keep it bottled up inside. The memory of his indifference to Maxime's death chilled her to the bone. This time, Milo brooded and grew more miserable as the days went by. He lost interest in school, refusing to play at recess. He looked sadder and sadder and began to lose his appetite.

David and Laetitia had never taken Justine Philippot up on her suggestion of family therapy, but now they had second thoughts. Milo clearly needed help, and they, too, could use some support to face the future with optimism. Laetitia was sleeping badly; her nights were crowded with worrying dreams that haunted her with absurd images that she tried in vain to decipher when sleep deserted her in the small hours. As the days passed, she realized that her outlook on life had been changed for the worse by the two tragedies. She was fearful, permanently on high alert. She quivered whenever the phone rang, convinced it would be news of another disaster, and jumped at every unexpected noise at home, at work, and on the street.

Above all, she became obsessed with Milo's safety. She hovered over him all day long, not daring to leave him alone for a second, watching him every minute, warning him to be careful, terrified he would hurt himself.

David felt more or less the same, but expressed it very differently. Inwardly. Aggressively. The defenses he had developed as an unwanted child and on the streets as a teenager returned with a vengeance, dominating his reflexes. His suspicions over Ernest's death gnawed at him. Why had his friend died just a short walk away from their house? His mind ran wild, picturing the worst. The past sometimes has the unfortunate habit of intruding on the present.

Gradually, his old demons stirred back to life.

And first in the firing line was Milo, exposed to the negative atmosphere at home and absorbing all his parents' unhealthy emotions. To begin with, he stubbornly refused to obey his mother. The perpetual pressure of her hovering over him made him reject all attempts at discipline. He said no to everything, began to talk back, and complained constantly. He grew afraid of his father's newfound temper. Laetitia couldn't cope with Milo when it was just the two of them, but as soon as his father came home he was cowed into obedience. Their house was drained of joy and laughter. Their family bond was at breaking point.

They went back to see Justine Philippot.

"So let me just recap. You came to see me last time because you thought your child was not expressing his grief enough. And now you've come to see me because you're worried he's expressing it too much."

David and Laetitia exchanged embarrassed glances.

"This time, I'd like to talk to Milo alone," Justine said. "You can wait next door."

They nodded, stood up, and left.

"I feel like a bad student thrown out of class for not doing my homework." Laetitia sighed, choosing a chair in the tiny waiting room.

"Well, that's true in a way," grumbled David.

Laetitia looked intrigued. He continued, "If we'd done a better job as parents, we wouldn't be here."

It struck Laetitia that David saw the need for family therapy as a failing. She was briefly tempted to reason with him, to soften the bitter defeat and his sense of powerlessness. But she said nothing. What was the point?

They sat, silent and brooding, for an hour. At long last, the door opened and Justine motioned for them to come back into her office. Milo was sitting in what had been Laetitia's chair, leaning busily over the table and drawing. Justine drew up another chair and gestured to the parents to sit down. When they were all settled in, she was the first to speak.

"Can you tell me exactly how, when, and where Ernest died?"

Justine made this sound like a question, but it was obvious it was more of a demand for the detailed truth. David and Laetitia exchanged glances again. This time their eyes were full of worry, which Justine picked up on.

David gave her a succinct account of events on Milo's birthday. Ernest had come to the party, left around four thirty, and his body was found at the end of the street three hours later.

"How did he die?"

"Heart attack," Laetitia immediately responded.

"Do you feel responsible for your friend's death?"

"Absolutely not!" David and Laetitia exclaimed in chorus.

Justine turned to Milo.

"There you go, Milo. Does that answer your questions?"

Milo, who had been drawing all the time, at long last looked up from his paper. He gazed at Justine for a moment, then gave a furtive nod.

"Do you have any other questions for your parents?"

He thought for a few seconds, then asked, "What's a heart attack?"

Laetitia understood then that most of the session must have been about what she and David were trying to keep from Milo. Quickly, she said, "Sometimes, when people get old or are in poor health, their hearts suddenly stop beating. That's what we call a heart attack."

She gave Milo time to react, maybe even ask another question. He said nothing, so she continued, "Milo, do you think that Dad and I haven't explained enough what happened to Ernest?"

Eyes downcast, as if he refused to look his mother in the face, Milo merely shrugged.

"Milo, look at me," she gently insisted.

He just looked down at his paper and boldly drew four thick lines in the shape of two Xs. Then he held the sheet out to Justine. She took it and studied it carefully. Then, wordlessly, she placed it on the desk in front of David and Laetitia.

The drawing was of five people in a line. The first was a little boy who had to be Maxime, with his round blue-framed glasses. The second was Ernest, with a gray beard and hair sticking up in tufts. In the center was David, next to Laetitia. Finally, squished up against the edge of the sheet, another little boy. Milo. Making himself small, contrite, grateful for the small space allotted to him.

The two fat Xs were struck through Maxime and Ernest.

CHAPTER 39

That evening, back home after the draining psychotherapy session, Milo had his first accident. Laetitia was upstairs undressing him for his bath when the doorbell rang. David opened the door to find Tiphaine standing on the step, carrying a potted plant with pretty purple bell-shaped flowers in one hand and a wrapped present in the other.

She greeted David and said, "Surprise! I brought over Milo's birthday present. We're so sorry we missed the party . . . but it was too much for us to handle."

"I understand," said David, taking the present from her.

"And this is for Laetitia," Tiphaine continued, holding out the potted plant. "It's a foxglove. She can plant it in the yard or leave it in its pot on the terrace, either is fine. It was being thrown out at work and our yard is already full. It's pretty and it flowers all summer."

"Thank you—"

"And I have an offer you can't refuse. I've made a ton of couscous, ten times too much for us. Would you guys like to come over?"

Taken by surprise, David instinctively turned to see if Laetitia agreed, but she was upstairs.

"We'd love it if you could," Tiphaine added.

"OK . . . we'll be over as soon as Milo is out of the bath."

Tiphaine smiled gratefully. As she headed out the door, David handed her back the gift. "Here, you can give it to him yourself."

"Sounds good."

Clean and freshly shampooed, looking cute in his Superman PJs, Milo unwrapped a magnificent Hot Wheels track from his godmother, a gift that made even Sylvain and David envious. They quickly volunteered to help the little boy set it up.

"You don't need to get everything out this evening," Laetitia intervened. "If you want to play with it tomorrow morning, we'll set it up at home."

"He can sleep over if he likes," Tiphaine suggested. "That way he can play while we have a drink and then when he wakes up tomorrow he can stay and play with it for as long as he likes."

Milo nodded enthusiastically. "Oh yes, Mom, please! Can I sleep over?"

David and Laetitia exchanged glances. Laetitia was still not entirely comfortable with Tiphaine, though she felt slightly guilty about it.

"Where . . . which room would he sleep in?" she asked, fearful of the answer.

"In the guest room," Tiphaine said, as if it were obvious.

"The guest room?"

"We've turned Maxime's room into a guest room," she explained simply. "All ready for its first guest."

Sylvain ruffled Milo's neatly combed hair. "And who better to test it out than our good friend Milo, am I right?"

"He's more than just a friend," Tiphaine added quietly.

An embarrassed silence settled over the group at the thought of Milo sleeping in what had once been Maxime's bed. Laetitia repressed an icy shiver and her heart began thumping. She was about to refuse when Milo began begging.

"Please, Mom, can I sleep over? Please?"

Milo's eagerness threw her off, breaking down her reluctance. Awkward and indecisive, she turned to Tiphaine and Sylvain to try and buy some time. "Are you guys sure?"

"You know what we think about it," Tiphaine assured her, with just a hint of irritation.

The situation was becoming ridiculous. So much hesitation over something that just a few months before would have been a perfectly natural request was souring the atmosphere. David stepped in, ignoring Laetitia's clumsy attempts to get out of it.

"Of course you can sleep over, big man!" he exclaimed.

Milo shrieked with delight and immediately started opening the Hot Wheels box. The subject was closed. Laetitia gave a somewhat forced smile.

Tiphaine and Sylvain seemed at ease. Or at least they were clearly striving to seem relaxed, trying to make the evening a pleasant one. But the atmosphere turned somber when David and Laetitia had to break the news of Ernest's death.

Tiphaine and Sylvain could not mask their dismay. They asked about the circumstances of the tragedy, commenting on the details and spotting the gap in Ernest's afternoon, just as

David and Laetitia had. They asked how they were holding up and how Milo had taken the news.

"It's not exactly the happiest of times for us," Laetitia admitted, lowering her voice so that Milo could not overhear her. "Let's just say there's been a lot . . ."

She fell silent, realizing how inappropriate she sounded: it was downright indecent to complain about tough times to parents who had just lost their only child. Ashamed of her own pain, she looked up at Tiphaine and Sylvain in embarrassment, and was staggered to see a strength in their gaze that rooted her to the spot. It was as if their roles had suddenly been switched.

She felt even worse when Tiphaine held out a friendly hand to comfort her. The gesture clearly meant "Don't worry, I'm here for you. I know what it's like to hurt. I've been there." Yet it seemed to Laetitia that their bereavement was far from over, as if the agony of such a great loss could never have faded in a few short months.

"How do you do it?" she murmured, trying hard to blink away her tears.

David came over and gave her a discreet hug. It was meant as moral support but was seen as a hint for Laetitia to pull herself together. For a moment, everyone looked apologetic: the Brunelles for being too sad, the Geniots for not being sad enough. Then Milo's imperious little voice snapped them out of the awkward silence, demanding attention and clamoring to play with his gift. They all reacted with relief to his interruption, and time, which seemed to have stood still, began ticking on.

As the men studied the Hot Wheels track instructions, Tiphaine and Laetitia prepared the refreshments in the kitchen, chatting about this and that. Tiphaine told Laetitia about the ongoing rivalry and tension between two of her colleagues, which she found difficult to deal with. Laetitia half-listened, realizing after a while that she was subconsciously still looking for an excuse to take Milo home.

Exasperated at her own anxiety, she tried to brush away her ridiculous overprotective reaction and made an effort to relax.

"I bought some Doritos, especially for Milo," Tiphaine said, pointing to a bowl of chips on the kitchen side. "I know he loves them."

"That was kind of you."

Something about Tiphaine's comment bothered Laetitia. Hadn't she told David that they were welcome to come over for dinner because she'd made too much couscous? Clearly, the invitation was not as spontaneous as Tiphaine had made it out to be.

They each carried a tray of glasses, bottles, and snacks into the living room, placed it on the coffee table, and poured the drinks. The Hot Wheels track was nearly finished. Milo hovered over David and Sylvain like a lost soul, clearly wanting to join in. The two men seemed to be enjoying themselves immensely.

"Can't you let him help?" Tiphaine said, a note of reproach in her voice.

Laetitia giggled. "Two overgrown kids."

"Milo, fetch my glasses from the kitchen, kiddo. They're on the counter," said Sylvain. Thrilled to be asked, the boy sped out of the living room.

Tiphaine stared accusingly at Sylvain, who said, "What? You said I should let him help!"

"Ready for a drink?" Laetitia held out two glasses to David and Sylvain, who left the track and sat down around the coffee table. They all raised their drinks through force of habit, but no one proposed a toast. This was the first time the four of them had shared a moment of leisure since Maxime's death, and in Tiphaine and Sylvain's house. Were they all thinking about the little boy as they sipped their drinks in silence?

Milo burst back in, breaking the weirdly awkward atmosphere. He held out Sylvain's glasses. Sylvain took them with a word of thanks.

"Would you like something to drink, Milo?" asked Tiphaine. He shook his head.

"Look, I got you some Doritos," she said, holding out the bowl. "Just for you!"

"Chips!" exclaimed David, pretending to grab a handful. Tiphaine slapped his hand away. "Don't you dare!"

Milo let out a giggle.

"All for you, sweetie," she said, passing him the bowl.

He grabbed a handful and wandered over to the Hot Wheels track. The four adults kept drinking and chatting, carefully sticking to uncontroversial topics that, while on the boring side, at least steered clear of awkwardness. It was a tricky balancing act. Sylvain discussed the ups and downs of the housing market while a faintly bored Laetitia listened with feigned interest. It suddenly struck her that Maxime's death had taken away the main thing they had in common.

The thought bothered her. She told herself that their friendship predated their children . . . what did they talk about back then? And when Maxime was alive, did they only ever talk about the children? Of course not. So what was the problem? Laetitia realized that before, they had been on the same team, and now something had changed. The thought saddened her, but more than her own sense of loss, she realized that the tragedy that had befallen her friends had created an unbridgeable gulf between them. And the gulf would always be there. Forever.

Sadness is a burden that, unlike happiness, cannot be shared.

A moan of pain interrupted her thoughts, bringing her back to Tiphaine and Sylvain's living room with a jolt. David was now chatting about protecting threatened species: she had no idea how the conversation had moved on from the cost of mortgages to animal protection.

"Milo? Are you OK?"

The alarm in Tiphaine's voice sent Laetitia into an immediate panic. She turned to look at her son, who was bent double, clutching his stomach.

"Milo!"

In two strides she was by his side, seizing his arms with her hands. He writhed in agony, lifting to his mother a face that was pale and covered in sweat. A horrified Laetitia tried to hug him, but as she wrapped her arms around him he stiffened, racked with convulsions.

"What's wrong with him!" she screamed, overcome with terror. "Do something, for God's sake!"

Tiphaine stood in the middle of the room, rooted to the spot. David and Sylvain stood beside her, bewildered at the unexpected turn of events. Tiphaine suddenly dashed into the kitchen, returning within a few seconds. She rushed over to Laetitia, tore Milo from her arms, and stuck a finger down his throat.

"Call an ambulance, quick!" she barked at Sylvain.

Sylvain looked totally dumbstruck. He seemed to shake himself awake and lunged for the telephone to dial the emergency services.

As Tiphaine held him tight, Milo began to vomit.

CHAPTER 40

David and Laetitia waited nervously in the emergency room for news of Milo. He had been whisked off to a special room upon arrival and they were not allowed to go with him. After the frantic scramble to get him to the hospital, they found themselves alone and confused. The helplessness of not knowing what was happening to their child was sheer torment. Laetitia sat slumped on a chair, while David paced the corridor.

The ambulance had taken barely five minutes to respond to Sylvain's call and the paramedics had immediately pumped the little boy's stomach before hoisting him into the ambulance. David and Laetitia had hastily climbed in and the vehicle sped off, blue lights flashing. Milo groaned in pain all the way to the hospital, his eyes rolled back in his head and his body racked with spasms.

Laetitia watched in horror, convinced her son was dying before her very eyes.

Now all they had to do was wait. She went over and over the events of the evening in her mind, trying to understand. What could Milo have eaten to make him so sick? She could think of nothing dangerous he might have consumed. Yet one detail kept haunting her. As soon as the paramedics arrived,

Tiphaine insisted they pump Milo's stomach. One of the ambulance team had spoken to her briefly before telling his colleague to feed the tube down Milo's throat.

Clearly, Tiphaine knew something she didn't.

Laetitia clenched her teeth. Her mistrust and suspicion of her neighbor was growing.

Seeing Tiphaine come racing around the corner with Sylvain—they had followed the ambulance in their own car—she leaped to her feet and ran to meet them.

"What has he eaten?" she yelled even before Tiphaine and Sylvain reached her, her voice bouncing off the walls. "What have you done to him?"

"Let me explain, Laetitia," Tiphaine said defensively, waving her hands in front of her in an attempt to soothe her friend. "It was an accident. A terrible accident."

The words brought David dashing to Laetitia's side. The two couples stood facing each other. Tiphaine began to explain.

"You remember Sylvain asked Milo to fetch his glasses from the kitchen . . . He must have snuck a taste of one of my herbal remedies. Some are very toxic, at least at this stage of the preparation. I left them out on the side . . . He must have tried one, it's the only explanation I can think of. The poultice I was making today is for external use only, it's definitely not meant to be eaten!"

She was stammering and seemed extremely upset, but Laetitia didn't care.

"You *bitch*!" she screamed, throwing herself at Tiphaine. "You tried to kill my son! You can't bear seeing him alive, so you tried to get rid of him!" She battered Tiphaine with her fists, hurling terrible accusations at her. David gripped Laetitia by the shoulders and dragged her backward. Tiphaine, shielding her face with her arms, made no attempt to ward off the blows. Sylvain immediately stepped between the two women, trying to reason with Laetitia. "Calm down, for God's sake! You're talking nonsense!"

When the two women were separated, Tiphaine burst into tears.

"It was an accident," she moaned, half-collapsing. "It's not my fault, I swear. Just an accident . . ."

David was still gripping Laetitia by the shoulders, trying to turn her around and face him to calm her down. But she was too upset and beside herself with rage to listen.

"I don't believe you!" she roared, struggling to break free from David's iron grip. "You did it on purpose!"

"How can you say such a thing?" sobbed Tiphaine, terrified at the turn of events.

"How could *you* leave poison out where he could reach it?"

"I never meant to hurt him! I'd just finished . . ."

"You don't leave poison out where a child can reach it!" shouted Laetitia, refusing to listen. "*Everyone* knows that! You never meant to hurt him? So tell me, how did he manage to sneak a taste of your poison?"

Tiphaine, limp as a rag doll in Sylvain's arms, suddenly raised her head and stared at Laetitia with eyes full of pain.

"I don't pay as much mind to household risks these days, because I don't have a child living with me anymore!" she screamed, her voice breaking in agony.

A flash of disgust shot across Laetitia's face. She stopped

struggling, and in response David loosened his grip. Free from his viselike arms, she stood firm and shot Tiphaine a look of utter contempt.

"Wrong way around, Tiphaine," she corrected, her voice icy. "You don't have a child living with you anymore *because* you don't pay enough mind to household risks."

"That's *enough*!" barked Sylvain, horrified.

His shout froze the two women. Sylvain, his face a twisted mask of pain, let go of Tiphaine. She fell to her knees sobbing. He slowly stepped toward Laetitia and pointed at her threateningly, repeating, "That's *enough*, Laetitia. Shut up. Shut your mouth, or I'll shut it for you, you hypocritical little *bitch*."

Laetitia instinctively took a step backward. David moved in front of her, protecting her with his body. A hostile silence settled over the group, all staring at one another in disgust, bitterness, loathing, and grief. And a deep sense of mistrust. Their eyes were filled with the pain, doubt, and fear of the evening's events.

It was clear that their friendship, already on its last legs, was now over. For good.

David sighed. "Leave us alone now," he ordered, his voice flat. "Just go!"

The only sound was Tiphaine's sobs. The two men stood facing each other. Sylvain soon dropped his gaze. He slowly turned on his heel and helped Tiphaine to her feet. She leaned heavily on his arm as the two of them made for the exit.

CHAPTER 41

The wait went on, the seconds ticking away in a tangle of emotions, desperate hope giving way to pitiless anguish. The certainty of being safe from misfortune shatters inexorably, like a splinter being driven into your soul, leaving behind fissures that you try to repair because this sort of thing only happens to other people . . . And words and pictures come to mind and linger, cruel, unbearable. You close your eyes so as not to see, not to feel, not to think. Pathetic attempts to escape disaster by sheer force of will.

Laetitia slumped back down on a chair. David began pacing the corridor again. Time seemed to have come to a standstill in a kind of desert, a purgatory in which a judge's gavel might come smashing down at any moment with a single word. A courtroom. A torture chamber. A hospital waiting room.

Lost in thought, Laetitia suddenly realized she was holding her breath, as if to slow the passage of time and freeze it at a point where all options were still open. Was her little boy going to die? The very thought was inconceivable. And the slightest brush with the hell Tiphaine and Sylvain were living through shed new light on her understanding of the situation.

What she had said to Tiphaine, the accusations she had yelled without thinking, just lashing out, as if her own pain could be lessened by hurting her friend . . . it was her subconscious talking, she was sure of it.

Had Tiphaine tried to kill Milo?

Laetitia was really beginning to think so. The more she thought about it, the clearer and more lucid her train of thought seemed. How could Tiphaine bear the sight of Milo? He was the living image of her dead son, the child Maxime would never be, the perpetual memory of the boy she had lost.

The living accusation of the fault she had committed.

The two boys had been inseparable, and Tiphaine's memories of Maxime were irrevocably bound up with Milo. Despite her pain, Tiphaine must have faced the fact that she, and she alone, was responsible for her little boy's death. How could she survive with that terrible blade stabbing at her heart every moment, every microsecond of the day?

But the worst of all the torments Tiphaine and Sylvain faced on a daily basis must be seeing a joy that was now forever out of their grasp, on their very own doorstep. Being friends and neighbors had once been a blessing: it was now a torture that grew more agonizing by the day. Milo coming home from school. Milo playing in the yard. Milo's birthday. Milo's giggles. Milo growing up. Milo living his life! The inconceivable symbol of enchantment, slashed by the sword of guilt. Their neighbors living in paradise while they struggled in the depths of hell.

And since paradise was out of reach, their only hope of survival was to destroy it.

Yes, she was now sure Tiphaine had tried to kill Milo. This was no accident. She thought back to the pair of them chatting in the kitchen as they got the drinks ready. She could not recall a bowl of herbal remedy anywhere on the work surface. Tiphaine had said her concoctions were out on the side . . . but if they were, surely she would have seen them. How could Tiphaine have got Milo to take the poison?

"The Doritos!" she exclaimed, sitting up straight on her chair. David turned to her in surprise.

"What about them?"

"Tiphaine poisoned Milo!"

"What are you talking about?"

"Think! Tiphaine had the Doritos out in a bowl even before we started getting the drinks ready. And when you reached for some, she slapped your hand away. They were for Milo, she knows how much he loves them . . . I'm sure she put poison on them!"

"You are out of your goddamn mind!"

David seemed sure she was wrong. She was convinced that once she explained her train of thought, he would come around to her point of view. He would have to agree that their neighbors were now a threat and living next door was putting their child in ever greater danger.

Their former friendship—what had previously been their source of strength—was now the weakest point in their defenses.

Laetitia was about to explain her thinking to David when the door to Milo's room opened. A doctor came out.

"Are you Milo's parents?"

David and Laetitia nodded silently, holding their breath, with lumps in their throats.

"I am Dr. Ferreira. It's too soon to be absolutely sure, but it looks like your boy is out of danger."

CHAPTER 42

Driving home, Tiphaine could not stop whimpering, the sound echoing around the car like that of an animal in mortal pain. Sylvain stared darkly at the road, powerless to relieve his wife's distress.

"He'll be fine," he murmured as they waited at a red light.

"If he dies, I'll kill myself!" Tiphaine howled, head in hands.

"Don't say that . . ."

"I swear, if he dies, I'll kill myself!" she repeated in a tragic tone to show him she really meant it.

"He won't die."

Rain began to fall, streaking the windshield with delicate rivulets. The shimmer from the red traffic light softened to a warm glow inside the car. Sylvain switched on the wipers almost wearily. The regular swish kept time with Tiphaine's sobs, like a mocking metronome. Sylvain was about to speak, but seemed to think better of it and remained silent.

The light turned green.

"Maybe I'm just not up to looking after children," Tiphaine lamented in a barely audible whisper.

She stared into space, picturing the horror of Milo in a hospital bed, sick, dying.

"Maybe Laetitia is right not to trust me," she added anxiously.

"He'll be fine. I promise."

"Either way . . ."

"You're in shock, Tiphaine. Laetitia, too. It won't seem so bad tomorrow."

He put the car into gear and drove on.

CHAPTER 43

Milo came around a few hours later, though Dr. Ferreira insisted on keeping him in for forty-eight hours. He had ingested a few grams of a concoction containing autumn crocus, a highly toxic plant used to treat gout, that Tiphaine was making for her father. At least, that was what she explained to the paramedics when they arrived, to convince them Milo needed his stomach pumped right away. Autumn crocus contains colchicine, which has long been used as a diuretic, painkiller, and anti-inflammatory, but which is also highly toxic, even fatal, when ingested at even very low doses. Milo had swallowed only a tiny amount, but it put him at death's door.

David and Laetitia took turns sitting by Milo's bedside for forty-eight hours straight. As the hours passed, his color improved and he began to look a little better. As soon as he was well enough to talk, Laetitia asked him the question that had been torturing her. "Did you eat anything in Tiphaine's kitchen when you went to fetch Sylvain's glasses?"

Milo's face clouded over. He said nothing for several long seconds, then shook his head. Laetitia's heart began to race. Yet Milo's expression left her feeling doubtful. She knew her son. She knew what he looked like when he misbehaved.

"Milo, sweetheart, it's very important," she said gently. "I promise you're not in any trouble, but you have to tell the truth. Did you eat or drink anything when you were alone in Auntiphaine's kitchen?"

Laetitia's kind tone seemed to reassure Milo, who looked up and confessed sheepishly, "There was a bowl on the table. It looked like brown sugar, but a bit more yellow."

"And did you taste a little bit?"

"A tiny bit . . ."

"What did it taste like?"

"It was yucky. I spat it out in the sink."

Laetitia sighed. "Good job." Milo's confession confirmed Tiphaine's story, but Laetitia could not shake off her doubts. If Milo had spat the mixture out in the sink, how could he have been so sick? "Did you spit it *all* out, or did you swallow a tiny bit?"

"I don't remember."

Within twenty-four hours his appetite had returned, and two days later he was clamoring to go home. On the morning of day three, Dr. Ferreira signed the release forms, showering David and Laetitia with advice: in some cases, colchicine can cause illness for up to ten days after ingestion.

"Our tests show that Milo no longer has any colchicine in his system, but at the slightest hint of trouble with his digestive tract, heart, nerves, or breathing, you need to bring him straight back in without wasting a second. We'll give him a thorough checkup every four weeks, so I'll see you in a month."

David and Laetitia nodded and drove Milo home.

That evening, when Milo was in bed, Laetitia sat David down to explain her suspicions. She had spent hours mulling it over during the previous two days and it was absolutely settled in her mind: Tiphaine had tried to kill Milo deliberately. Maxime's death had been such a painful experience, it had clearly driven her mad—just look at the crazy accusations she flung at Laetitia for not saving her son's life and even blaming her outright for his death.

"And the big change in attitude after the funeral," she went on bitterly. "Doesn't that strike you as odd? They stubbornly refuse to speak to us, then, all of a sudden, they want to be best friends again."

"Tiphaine admitted she was wrong," David objected.

"Bullshit! It was the only way they could get close to Milo!"

"Come on, Laetitia, you don't really believe this, do you?"

Laetitia opened her eyes wide in astonishment. "What more proof do you need? She's been in contact with Milo twice since Maxime died, and both times his life has been in danger!"

"Twice?" he asked in surprise. "When was the first time?"

"For Christ's sake, David!" she snapped. "I spotted him leaning out Maxime's bedroom window! As if . . . as if she wanted the same thing to happen to him!"

David looked unconvinced, sending Laetitia into a towering rage.

"I don't get why you're not willing to look facts in the face. Milo is constant torture for her. Every time she sees or hears him, it brings it all back—Maxime and her own unforgivable mistake. Just a few steps away from her own front door! I mean, that must be sheer hell on earth to live with!"

"Calm down, Laetitia," David said soothingly. "I agree we need to cut contact with them from now on. But I don't believe Tiphaine would want to kill Milo."

"Really?" spat Laetitia, choking with anger. "How can you be so sure? Go on, tell me!"

David thought carefully before replying. "First off, Milo himself said he tasted some weird concoction that looked like brown sugar."

"Which he immediately spat out!" Laetitia jumped in.

"Maybe he did swallow some without realizing. And anyway, how could Tiphaine be sure Milo would taste the mix?"

"Of course she would be sure! I bet she put some on the Doritos. Milo said it was like brown sugar, but yellower. Doesn't that ring a bell?"

David looked perplexed.

"Exactly the color of Doritos, with all that yellow powder on them!" exclaimed Laetitia, as if that clinched it. "All she had to do was sprinkle some on the chips and no one would have been any the wiser. What she told the paramedics, that Milo must have sneaked a taste from one of her remedies, is bullshit!"

"But Milo *did* . . ."

"Yes, but that's not what made him sick."

"So, tell me, why did she try and save his life?"

Laetitia scoffed. "What did she do to save him?"

"She made him throw up, she yelled at Sylvain to call an ambulance, she told the paramedics to pump his stomach," David said calmly, ticking off each point on his fingers.

"Of course! If she didn't, she would have been top of the list of suspects in a murder case and she'd have spent the rest of her life behind bars! But by pretending to want to save him, it just looks like a household accident. Just sheer bad luck."

David had no comeback to that. He looked baffled.

"I've done my homework, David," Laetitia continued, determined as ever. "Autumn crocus is a very strong poison that triggers spontaneous vomiting, and it's usually fatal."

"So how come Milo survived?"

"Because he only swallowed a tiny amount! Her plan went wrong, that's all!"

David was again silent. Some of Laetitia's points were hitting home, yet he was not wholly convinced.

Out of arguments, Laetitia declared, "Anyway, he is *never* going anywhere near her ever again."

"Fine by me."

"But you don't believe me when I tell you she tried to kill him."

David sighed. "No, I don't. I know Tiphaine, and I don't think she's capable of such a thing."

Laetitia clenched her teeth and stood up to spit out her bitter words, looking down at David in contempt.

"Listen to me, David. If our son *ever* finds himself in danger again because of your stupid blind trust, I will hold you *personally* responsible."

She stalked from the room without looking back.

CHAPTER 44

Tiphaine had recently taken up jogging. She ran with no reason other than the need to feel herself moving, pounding straight ahead with no goal in mind. Just pure sensation. The new habit gave her the feeling of finding her footing in a reality that still had no flavor. And running stopped her from thinking. She just kept putting one foot in front of the other, plowing on, staring at the end of the road as if she had a goal in mind and letting her legs do the rest. She had no expectations. Just around the block, again and again. Dilapidate her strength, expend her energy, experience physical exhaustion in the hope that when she got home, her tired body would stop her tired mind from racing. After a run, her nights were usually less haunted. And that suited her perfectly.

That day, finishing her twelfth lap, she spotted Laetitia in the distance. She was getting out of her car, arms full of groceries, struggling to open Milo's door. Tiphaine stopped dead, tempted for a second to turn on her heel and run the other way. To avoid the confrontation, hide around the corner, wait for the coast to clear. But when she saw Milo clamber out of the car, eyes glued to his Nintendo, her heart beat faster, and it wasn't due to the physical exertion.

Without thinking, she began running again.

This time, her feet took her in a specific direction, and though it was just a short distance, she had no idea what lay before her. Could they be friends again? Unlikely. But she could convince Laetitia of her honesty. Or at least she could try. Even if she knew deep down inside it was a hopeless effort.

As she reached them, she heard Laetitia talking to Milo. "And shut the door, if it's not too much to ask!"

She sounded irritated, like she was in a bad mood. Was now a good time to try? The opportunity was there, at least, and Tiphaine decided to grab it.

"Laetitia! Do you have a moment?"

Laetitia turned around. Her expression was an unyielding blend of astonishment and mistrust. Time seemed to stand still. Before Laetitia could gather her wits to speak, Tiphaine stepped over to Milo and ruffled his hair.

"You doing OK, big guy?" His smile warmed her heart.

"Hi, Auntiphaine!"

His greeting seemed to shock Laetitia into action. She strode over angrily, grabbed her son's arm, and pulled him behind her.

"Don't you *dare* talk to him!" she hissed.

Tiphaine barely flinched.

"Laetitia, please, can we at least talk?"

"Get inside, Milo!" Laetitia ordered.

"But Mom . . ."

"Now!" Her tone told him not to push his luck. After a moment's hesitation, Milo went inside, pouting. Laetitia turned back to Tiphaine:

"Now you listen to me, you crazy bitch. If I see you anywhere near my son again, I'll scratch your eyes out."

The words killed off any lingering hope that Laetitia would ever change her mind. Tiphaine had been stupid to think it was possible. But now the two women were standing there, face-to-face, she had to say *something*.

"Listen, Laetitia, can't you understand that I never wanted . . ."

"Shut your mouth!" she hissed, eyes screwed tight in an exasperated scowl. "Keep your pathetic excuses to yourself. You don't fool me for one second!"

"Really? What *is* your take, then?"

Laetitia gave her a look of utter scorn.

"I know *exactly* what the hell you're trying to do, Tiphaine. But I warn you, if anything—*anything*—happens to my son, I'll call the cops on you."

Tiphaine was aghast. She had no idea that Laetitia had lost her grip on reality so completely. The seriousness of her allegation terrified her.

"I don't know what crazy thoughts have got into your head, Laetitia, but I promise you one thing: you're wrong. Please, just try to believe me. Not for my sake, but for Milo's. Because you're destroying him, bit by bit."

Laetitia arched one eyebrow, a look of contempt on her face. A cruel gleam flashed in her eyes like a lightning bolt in a stormy sky.

"Well, I guess you *do* know all about destroying children," she shot back, her voice almost silky.

The cruelty of the insinuation blinded Tiphaine with hideous pain that tore away her last scraps of self-control. She slapped Laetitia, hard. Instinctively.

Laetitia stood stunned for a moment, eyes wide with shock. The groceries and bags sawing at her fingers seemed to weigh several tons. She dropped them to raise one hand to her cheek.

"How *dare* you!" Tiphaine raged, choking back tears.

Tiphaine could tell Laetitia was ready to jump on her and scratch her eyes out. The air crackling with hatred. A voice rang out, interrupting the fight before it started.

"Laetitia!"

David rushed out of the house, grabbed Laetitia by the shoulders, and pushed her behind him protectively.

"She hit me!" she blurted, still in shock.

"B-but some words hurt worse," Tiphaine stammered, aghast at the turn the confrontation had taken.

David gave her a withering stare, weighing his words carefully as he pointed at her with a threatening finger. "You've gone too far this time, Tiphaine. We'll be reporting this."

Tiphaine knew there was nothing more she could do. They could never be civil to each other again.

"Fine, David. You do that. You see, the big difference between us now is that I have nothing left to lose."

CHILD MEDICAL RECORD

AGE 7–8

Your child will benefit from extracurricular activities, but leave them some free time for play.

> M. is reluctant to sign up for any after-school clubs . . . Should we force him? Maybe he'd like aikido, theater club, drawing, music?

> Too much Nintendo! Something to keep an eye on.

Mealtimes can be a great opportunity to ask about your child's day at school. Try switching off the TV to eat together.

> No TV in the kitchen. M. has a good appetite and enjoys talking about what happens at school. We have a very strong relationship.

DOCTOR'S NOTES:

Weight:___. Height: ___.

CHAPTER 45

The days were growing shorter, though the fall weather was still mild that year. In the week following the clash, the two couples did not cross paths. Living right next to each other, once such a delight, was a sword of Damocles over their heads now they risked bumping into each other whenever they stepped outside their front door. Even knowing the other couple was in their yard, just a few steps away, cast a long, bitter shadow of mistrust over their daily lives.

The following Saturday, Laetitia spent most of the morning catching up with the laundry, washing several loads and then ironing, folding, and putting away the clothes that had been drying on the rack. David was on his shift, driving around in his taxi. Milo, having watched his Jimmy Neutron DVD—he was allowed one hour of TV on Saturday mornings—asked if he could go out to play in the yard.

Laetitia agreed reluctantly. She didn't like her son being out where Tiphaine could see him: the house next door had a clear view of both yards from the upstairs windows. But it was ridiculous to stop Milo from playing outside, Laetitia knew that. She decided to set her ironing board up in the dining room, where the French windows opened onto the terrace and let her see the whole yard at a glance.

Milo's mood was still low, more so since he came out of the hospital. The ambiance at home was far gloomier than the cheery atmosphere that had once prevailed. Laetitia was on edge much of the time, which annoyed David, and they often argued. They had not said much to Milo about his hospital stay other than that he should never have dipped his finger in the yellowish sugar. But he knew perfectly well that his mother blamed Tiphaine for the accident and that David disagreed. Milo himself didn't know which of his parents to believe and he felt torn. He also genuinely liked Maxime's parents and was sad not to see them anymore. To cap it all off, he had asked for the Hot Wheels track several times, but it was still at their house.

"I'm sorry, sweetie, we can't," his mother said every time he asked.

"Why not?"

"If you really want a Hot Wheels track, Dad and I will buy you one."

That was the only answer he could get from her. But why he couldn't just fetch the one he already had remained a mystery. Knowing David's point of view, he tried asking him to explain.

"Your mom is very, very mad at Auntiphaine and doesn't want anything from her house."

"But it's not for her, it's for me!" Milo shouted. "It's *my* track!"

"I know, sweetheart."

"Will they stay mad forever and ever?"

David looked at Milo sadly and shrugged as if to say he had no idea.

That evening, in bed, Milo could hear shouting coming from downstairs. His parents were fighting again. Several times, he could make out the words *Hot Wheels*. He buried his face in his pillow and decided to give up hope of ever seeing the track again.

Busy with her ironing, Laetitia thought about her quarrel with David the night before. He had accused her of stressing Milo for no reason and convincing him to think he was in danger. It was unhealthy.

"But he *is* in danger!" she argued, desperate to persuade David that Milo's safety was at risk.

"Just *stop it*, for God's sake!" David bellowed. "You're completely paranoid! I mean, tell me, what possible risk could there be in Milo getting his track back?"

"I don't know," she admitted through gritted teeth.

David gave a triumphant smile, which faded as Laetitia added, "But one thing I *do* know is that Tiphaine is deranged enough to do something even to a Hot Wheels track. I mean, it does use electricity, after all."

David would have burst out laughing if the situation was not so miserably depressing.

"Frankly, *you* sound deranged!" he snapped back, pity in his eyes. His words cut Laetitia to the quick. She banged her fist on the table, venting her anger.

"Now you listen to me, David Brunelle. I don't get why you're trying to defend that . . . that *nutcase*. But don't you *dare* start insulting me! I won't stand for it!" She buried her face in her hands and burst into tears.

David could not mask his exasperation. He heaved a deep sigh and fought against the urge to storm out, slamming the door behind him. His wife's unhealthy need to wrap their son in cotton wool was beginning to get on his nerves. Most of all, he resented her for worrying Milo with her neuroses. The boy was upset enough about Maxime's and Ernest's deaths, and now he was losing his spark. He should be enjoying a carefree childhood. Didn't Laetitia realize her attitude was just making matters worse for her son, making him permanently miserable?

Seeing his wife in tears again, sad and vulnerable, David decided the time had come to break the infernal cycle she had become trapped in. What to do? He could see only one way out: force her to follow her own arguments to their logical conclusion.

"OK!" he said emphatically. "So you think Milo is in danger, right? Tiphaine is a real threat to him because she can't bear the thought of watching him grow up."

"It's blindingly obvious!" she sobbed.

"Well, then, we have to move!"

Laetitia was so shocked, her tears stopped. She stared at him in baffled astonishment. "What?"

"If you think our child is in danger here, next door to Tiphaine and Sylvain, well, our duty is to protect him. So let's move."

"Absolutely not!" she protested.

"Why on earth not?"

"This was my parents' house. I grew up between these four walls, and I want my son to do the same. I don't see why my neighbor going completely nuts should force me out of my home. If anyone should move, it should be her!"

"You can't force people to move just because you think their presence is a threat to your child. If you're so convinced you're right, then it's up to you to take the next step."

It was irrefutable logic and Laetitia could not come up with anything to counter it. The urge to see the back of Tiphaine and Sylvain once and for all swept over her with almost desperate strength.

"It's not fair," she wailed, her eyes brimming with tears again.

"Maybe. But that's the way it is."

She lost herself in painful thought, sniffing and sobbing occasionally.

Move to a new house? Leave the home that held so many memories of her own childhood, her son, her parents? Take Milo away from these familiar streets, maybe even change his school? And where would they go? Thinking through the implications, she realized she was far from ready to contemplate such a radical solution.

"Well, if the idea doesn't sound like a no-brainer, then maybe Milo isn't in as much danger as you seem to think . . . ," concluded David, who seemed to be reading her like an open book.

Laetitia barked a short, sardonic laugh. "You just want to prove me wrong, don't you?"

"I want to prove you are overthinking, and deep down,

you know it. OK, so Tiphaine isn't quite right in the head, but honestly, Laetitia, can you blame her? She's lost her son! She'll never get over it. Of course I agree with you that we cannot put Milo at any risk. We'll never see or speak to Tiphaine and Sylvain again, and that's that. But you can't go around thinking she's trying to harm him! And please, you have *got* to stop putting the thought into Milo's head. *You're* the one harming him right now. So please, drop the paranoia and let's both try to put a smile back on our boy's face!"

David's words hit home. The tears down Laetitia's cheeks ran twice as fast. She stood up, walked around the table, and nestled into David's arms, wordlessly smothering him in kisses.

The end of her reminiscing coincided with the end of her task. She folded the last pair of pants, put them on top of the pile and unplugged the iron. She saw Milo silhouetted at the end of the yard, busy playing. Grabbing the basket, she lugged it upstairs to put the clothes away carefully and change Milo's sheets. It took her about ten minutes. She headed back downstairs into the kitchen for a glass of water.

As she drank, she glanced casually out of the window at the yard. Lost in thought, she did not notice anything amiss. Only when she put the glass down in the sink did her instinct kick in. Something was wrong.

CHAPTER 46

Laetitia dashed out through the dining room onto the terrace to scan the yard in a single glance. "Milo?"

She hurried down to the shrubs at the far end, calling his name, and poked around in the hedge. "Milo, if you're hiding, come on out! It's not funny!"

Turning around, she looked back over the lawn and terrace. "Milo! For god's sake, where are you?"

Next she tore open the shed door. "Milo?" She froze, panting and trying to choke down a rising tide of panic. The shed held just the usual tools, lawn mower, and a few sacks of topsoil piled in a corner. Nowhere for a boy to hide. Heart pounding, she spun around and stared at the end of the hedge, where Milo and Maxime had created a tunnel months before. Not even bothering to close the shed door, she raced over, knelt down, and peered through the narrow opening.

No sign of Milo anywhere.

Fighting panic, she got up and stood on tiptoe to look over the hedge. Tiphaine and Sylvain's yard was much more generously planted than hers, but she couldn't see anything moving.

She had to face facts. Milo was not in the yard.

Had he sneaked inside while she was upstairs? She dashed

back into the dining room and searched the ground-floor rooms, screaming his name. Then she went upstairs, flinging open the bedroom doors. She did not take the time to look in the closets or under the beds. Somehow, her instinct was telling her Milo was not there. Running out of ideas—or warding off the one terrifying thought crowding her mind—she ran back downstairs and out the front door.

The street was empty, save for the cars that zoomed by every few seconds, indifferent to her panic, vanishing as swiftly as they had appeared.

Terror was keeping her from thinking straight. She hesitated on the sidewalk, her tortured thoughts obsessed with the certainty that something had happened to her precious boy.

"That *bitch*!" she muttered, striding to the house next door.

She mashed her finger on the doorbell, waited, then started again. When no one answered, she hammered on the door. "I know you're there, Tiphaine!" she bellowed at the top of her lungs. "Open the door, or I'm calling the police!"

She held her ear to the door to try to hear if anyone was inside.

Total silence.

Laetitia felt the last shreds of self-control slip from her grasp. In the grip of nameless panic, she sprinted home, threw herself at the phone, and called David. When he picked up, she was in tears.

It took him a while to understand what was going on. Laetitia's explanation was muddled. She said Milo was gone, but he could not understand how. She accused Tiphaine of kidnapping her son and threatened to break in next door to save him.

"Calm down, Laetitia, for the love of God!" David tried to soothe her, trying to inject a sense of calm reason into his voice. "What makes you think Tiphaine and Sylvain have him?"

"He was in the yard, David! The only place he can have gone is through the hedge. There's nowhere else he can be!"

"Why would he go to theirs?"

"Don't you *get* it?" shrieked Laetitia, on the verge of hysteria. "She *lured* him in with some horrible trick. I have to get into their house, or we'll never see Milo again!"

"Don't you *dare* do that!" shouted David, losing his temper in turn. "Don't move. Actually, call the police, tell them Milo is missing, and wait. I'm on my way."

He stabbed at the off button, dropped the phone on the passenger seat, and parked the car. Turning to the man who had just got into his taxi, he apologetically asked him to get out again.

"Is this some kind of joke?" protested the client, visibly irritated.

"I'm very sorry, sir . . . that was my wife. Something has happened to my son. I have to get home right now."

Anyone reasonable would have done what he asked. Unfortunately, the client seemed not to care for children.

"Not my problem!" he snapped. "Take me where I want to go and then you're free to do whatever you want."

David could tell he was dealing with an asshole. Time was of the essence and every second wasted trying to persuade the client to get out was making him more annoyed. He heaved an audible sigh, turned off the ignition, and got out of the taxi.

He stalked around to the back passenger door and yanked it open. "Out!"

"Absolutely not!" said the client, clutching his briefcase as if it were anchoring him to the back seat.

Not stopping to think, David grabbed him by the lapel and hauled him out of the car by brute force. The man tried to resist, shouting in protest and leaning away from David like a deadweight until David had to let go. David was losing patience. He tried again, with both hands this time, and dragged the man out of the car till he fell down on all fours. David let go and the man slumped to the ground.

David did not look back. He got in behind the wheel, turned the key, and sped off. Glancing in the rearview mirror, he saw the client climb to his feet, yelling what looked like terrible insults after him. Or maybe threats. Five minutes later, David braked hard outside the house, tires squealing, and hurried in. He found Laetitia on her knees in the hall, feverishly pawing through the strewn contents of the chest of drawers.

"What the hell are you doing?" he asked in astonishment.

"Looking for those damn keys!" she screeched, not even looking up.

"What keys?"

"The keys to Tiphaine and Sylvain's house!"

"Did you call the police?"

"They'll be here any second."

David stood silent for a few seconds, watching his wife grab random items from the scattered mess on the floor and toss them aside.

"*Stop it*, Laetitia!" he barked. "Calm down and tell me what happened."

She said nothing. She carried on searching, picking things up, casting them aside, groaning, swearing, and wiping her tears on her sleeve.

"For Christ's sake, Laetitia, that's *enough*!" he screeched, his nerves shattered.

Laetitia jumped and looked up at him, her eyes full of distress. He grabbed her by the shoulders and pulled her to her feet. She let herself be guided by his powerful hands, falling into his arms and sobbing until her tears ran dry.

"So, do you want to tell me what's going on?" he asked her gently.

CHAPTER 47

There wasn't much to explain. Laetitia recounted the morning's events, focusing on the ten or so minutes when she had left Milo playing alone outside. The last time she saw him, he was at the far end of the yard. Then he was gone.

"Children don't just vanish!" murmured a baffled David. "He must be somewhere!"

"He's there!" spat Laetitia, pointing at Tiphaine and Sylvain's house. "God knows what she's doing to him! And you . . ."

She tore herself from David's arms, suddenly revolted. While he tried to hug her close, she shoved him away and pointed at him accusingly as he gazed at her in surprise. "You wouldn't believe me. I *told* you she wanted to hurt him. And now . . . now . . ."

She fell silent with a sharp sigh of pain, her eyes full of bitterness and anger, then suddenly raced back out to the terrace, David hot on her heels. She grabbed a chair and dragged it over to the hedge, just as she had done when she'd spotted Milo at Maxime's bedroom window and been filled with horror. As she clambered onto the chair, David tackled her, yelling, "Laetitia! What the hell are you doing?"

"Let me go!" she screeched, struggling to free herself.

Precariously balanced on the chair, she flung one leg over the hedge and lashed out at David with her other foot, catching him on the chest. It didn't hurt, but it did knock him off balance, and he was forced to let her go. She threw her other leg over and dropped down onto the terrace next door. Not wasting a second, she stood up and dashed over to try the sliding glass doors by Tiphaine and Sylvain's kitchen window. Locked. Heedless of David's shouts from behind the hedge as he tried to reason with her, she grabbed a wooden stool that stood on the side of the terrace.

"Laetitia, no!"

She brandished it above her head . . .

"Drop the stool!"

. . . and brought it crashing down on the glass door.

The expensive double glazing withstood the blow, leaving just a half-inch-long crack at the point of contact.

David was climbing over the hedge now, barking orders and shouting threats. Laetitia was deaf to his words. As she stood poised with the stool high over her head, she heard the sound of their own doorbell carrying through the open windows. She and David froze, staring at each other in panic.

"The police!" David exclaimed, remembering that Laetitia had called them.

That caught Laetitia's attention, cutting through her blind rage and bringing her hope that she might soon gain entry to the house next door—where, she was convinced, her child was being held captive.

She dropped the stool.

David was able to breathe again. He ordered her back into their own yard. Seeing her head for the hedge, he jumped down from the chair and went to open the front door.

Two uniformed officers stood on the threshold. The man proudly sported a large, well-groomed mustache. He was tall, bronzed, and square-jawed, and the sunglasses perched high on his nose made him look like a pale, less charismatic copy of Tom Selleck. The woman was nearly as tall, with ample curves. Her graying hair was cut short in a neat, practical style.

"Lieutenant Chapuy and Lieutenant Delaunoy," the man said. David did not grasp which name was which, and he didn't care. "You called about a missing child?"

David nodded. "Come in."

The two officers stepped inside as Laetitia came in through the kitchen, her clothes in disarray and hair sticking out in tufts.

"Thank God you're here!" she exclaimed. "The neighbors have taken my son prisoner, he's in serious danger! You have to break their door down, she is refusing to open up!"

"OK, slow down!" urged the female officer in a firm yet kind voice. "We need a full account of what's happened. Start with telling us about your son, then how he went missing."

Disappointed by what she saw as a waste of time, Laetitia was on the verge of answering back when David spoke up.

"Laetitia, just be quiet and let me explain! We have no proof Milo is at Tiphaine and Sylvain's."

"Milo is your son, is that right?" the officer asked.

"He's my boy. He's seven. And the neighbors have abducted him!" Laetitia snapped in a voice that betrayed her scathing assessment of their efficiency.

"I'm going to need you to calm down, madam," the Tom Selleck lookalike intervened. "We can't get started until we have the background details. It's in your own interest to get a grip and give us a detailed account of what happened and when exactly your son went missing. The faster we get started, the faster we can start the search."

"Let's go to the dining room," David suggested. He gestured to the two officers to sit down. Laetitia followed them, making a superhuman effort to keep calm. When they were all settled around the table, she told them once again what had happened. Then David briefly filled in the background of their relationship with their neighbors and why Laetitia was convinced Tiphaine was involved. The police officers took notes and asked plenty of follow-up questions.

"Have you searched the area and asked your other neighbors? Checked the local stores? Asked around in the streets?"

David and Laetitia shook their heads.

"Well, that's where we'll start," said the Tom Selleck cop, standing up. "Can you give us a recent photo?"

The other officer held her hand up for him to wait. She had another question. "Do you share your wife's suspicions about your neighbors?" she asked David.

He glanced at Laetitia, who returned him a threatening stare. He knew that she would take a no as a betrayal.

"Let's just say I don't trust Tiphaine much," he replied carefully. "But I'm not sure I'd say she's capable of anything so terrible."

Laetitia barked a short, sardonic laugh and looked away, her posture full of scorn. The police officers didn't comment on this, instead focusing on the information they needed. "Have you rung their bell?"

"No one answered," David answered hastily, thinking it better not to mention Laetitia's uninvited visit to their yard.

"I'm not crazy, you know!" said Laetitia in towering indignation.

No one reacted.

"Does your son have any special friends, people he knows, a favorite place he might have gone on his own initiative, without asking?"

"He's only seven!" exclaimed Laetitia, her voice cracking in a sob. "What will it take for you to understand time is of the essence? While we're sitting here talking pointlessly, Milo is in danger a few steps away, just on the other side of this wall . . ."

"Calm down, madam," soothed the policewoman. "I can promise you we're doing everything we can to locate your little boy."

As if to drive the message home, she again asked for a photograph. While her colleague went out to the car to radio in Milo's description, she conducted a quick search of the yard. From David and Laetitia's account of events and the circumstances, Delaunoy and Chapuy had swiftly decided to start with two main hypotheses. Either Laetitia was right and Milo had climbed through the hedge into next door's yard and was in the adjoining house, or he had gone out on his own for some reason without bothering to warn his parents, and was out wandering the streets. The two officers clearly judged that abduction by a stranger was unlikely: the yard could not be seen or reached from the street and it was highly improbable that anyone could have sneaked in at the precise moment when Laetitia was upstairs, crept to the far end of the yard undetected, grabbed the child, and got out without being seen.

Since the policewoman had found nothing of interest in the yard and her colleague had finished radioing Milo's description, they decided to start by ringing on Tiphaine and Sylvain's bell, with David and Laetitia hot on their heels.

The Tom Selleck cop pressed firmly on the doorbell and hammered on the door.

"Police! I need you to open the door!" he called in an authoritarian tone.

No response.

"We can go around the back," Laetitia suggested.

"Around the back?" the Tom Selleck cop asked in surprise. "What for?"

"To get inside and search the house!" she said, as if it was a no-brainer.

"It's far too early to be searching anyone's house, madam," he said. Seeing the crushing disappointment on her face, he added, "We can only search a private home when conducting preliminary inquiries, when we catch someone in the process of committing an offense, or with a search warrant. None of those apply in this case."

"So you're just going to stand here and do nothing?"

"We will do everything possible, madam. Within the limits of the law."

Laetitia felt on the verge of collapse. She looked over at David with eyes both devastated and accusatory, clearly blaming him for the police officers' lack of action and the laws they had to obey. As if this final obstacle had snapped something deep inside her, she threw herself at Tiphaine and Sylvain's front door, banging on it with her fists and screeching insults and threats at Tiphaine and comforting words for Milo, promising he would soon be free.

David had to intervene to try to calm her down once again, but she pushed him away as she would anyone who tried to get through to her. Crazed with pain and lost in the utter certainty of her conviction that her son was inside, just a few feet away on the other side of the door, she felt more terrifyingly lonely than she ever had before. She cursed the whole world, the source of all her miseries.

David pinned her in his arms and dragged her away from the door as she struggled furiously, howling and screaming at the top of her voice. The policewoman also tried to reason with her, but to no avail. Laetitia seemed to have lost her grip on reality and was now deaf to all attempts to calm her down.

"Look!" David suddenly called, trying to catch her attention.

He grabbed her firmly by the wrists to try to spin her around, holding her close to force her to look at him. But it was useless. She was beyond listening, beyond reason. He had to shake her violently to shut her up.

"*Look*, for God's sake!" he barked. More shocked than hurt, Laetitia at long last fell silent.

Following his gaze, she saw a familiar figure at the end of the street. Tiphaine was just coming home.

CHAPTER 48

Laetitia was stunned to see Tiphaine strolling along the side-walk, but Tiphaine was even more taken aback to see her neighbors at her front door with two police officers. Her arrival instantly brought Laetitia back to her senses. She wriggled free of David's arms and sprinted off down the street.

"What have you done to my son?" she shouted as soon as Tiphaine was within earshot.

David and the two officers were hot on her heels. David grabbed her arm, begging her to let Delaunoy and Chapuy do their job. He dragged her away as the Tom Selleck cop and his colleague approached Tiphaine, who was gaping at them with naked astonishment.

David and Laetitia watched the trio talking from a safe distance. Tiphaine shook her head and shrugged several times, appearing to answer their questions with short two- or three-word answers. Then all three headed for the house. As Tiphaine slipped her key into the lock, David and Laetitia hurried over.

"I'll let you look around my house, but no way is that crazy woman stepping foot in here," Tiphaine declared, pausing with the key turned halfway.

The policewoman turned around to face Laetitia, and said

quickly, "Mrs. Geniot is letting us inside, which she could perfectly well refuse to do according to the law. Lieutenant Delaunoy and I will look around, but I am asking you to wait outside."

This told David that the Tom Selleck lookalike was Delaunoy. Seeing Laetitia about to argue, Chapuy held up her hand. The message was clear: no negotiating. "And I don't want any complaints!" she snapped.

Laetitia swallowed her words and Chapuy turned back to Tiphaine, who turned the key completely. Pushing open the door, she stepped to one side to let the officers in first. As the door swung shut, she looked at Laetitia with fathomless pity in her eyes.

David and Laetitia went to wait on their own front step. A good twenty minutes went by in near complete silence. They swapped the occasional word, each hurt by the other's attitude and blaming each other for the sense of isolation that gnawed at them.

"He's not in there . . . ," muttered David reproachfully.

"If he's not in there, she must have had time to move him!"

Laetitia's response pushed David's nerves past their breaking point. "You are going freaking *insane*, Laetitia!" he hissed through clenched teeth. "And you are wasting precious time. We could be looking for Milo out there, wherever he is."

"Oh yeah? And where is he, in your opinion?"

Tiphaine and Sylvain's front door banged open and the two officers appeared, shaking Tiphaine's hand to thank her for cooperating.

"Not next door, anyway," David sighed bitterly.

He stood up, turning his back on Laetitia, and walked over to Chapuy and Delaunoy. They gave him a quick rundown: Tiphaine and Sylvain had nothing to do with Milo's disappearance, for the plain and simple reason that both had been at work since early that morning. Both had plenty of colleagues as eyewitnesses to account for their whereabouts all morning. The officers would be checking their alibis, but it all seemed perfectly straightforward. To be on the safe side they had conducted a thorough search of the house and yard, but as expected, they had found nothing suspicious.

David turned to Laetitia, who was still sitting on the front step. "Can we start looking for our son properly now?" he called, his exasperation clear for all to hear.

Laetitia remained impassive. She sat huddled, knees to her chest, staring into space at something only she could see.

"OK!" declared Delaunoy. "Enough time wasted! We'll look around the neighborhood and talk to anyone who might have seen him. We'll ask in stores and check with the other neighbors."

Tiphaine opened her door again and stuck her head out. She was clearly very upset. "I'll help with the search!" she offered, her voice quavering.

"Thank you, I'm sure we can use all the help we can get," Delaunoy replied. He glanced at his watch. "If the boy isn't back in fifteen minutes, we'll send out a missing child alert."

Chapuy nodded and walked over to Laetitia, still huddled on the step. "Mrs. Brunelle, if you want Milo back, we are going to need your help," she murmured kindly. "I know how hard it is, but sitting there isn't helping. The best way to . . ."

Delaunoy's walkie-talkie crackled, interrupting her. He stepped away from the little group, exchanged a few words with the muted, nasal voice at the other end, and called over, "A male child aged around seven has been found wandering alone on Rue du Marché-aux-Poissons, about half a mile away!"

Laetitia, David, and Tiphaine were by his side in an instant. Not wasting a second, Delaunoy spoke into the walkie-talkie, asking, "Can you give me his name?"

All three of them heard the answer together: "Milo Brunelle! His name's Milo Brunelle."

Fifteen minutes later, Laetitia was hugging her son tight.

CHAPTER 49

Life has changed. It was better before.

More fun.

I had Maxime, but that's not all. Back then, Auntiphaine and Sylvain were still friends with Mom and Dad. And that was great. Because when they were all together chatting and laughing, they didn't care what we got up to.

Maxime and me.

It's not like we could misbehave as much as we liked, but we did some stuff they never found out about. Like the time we farted on Mom and Dad's pillows. We laughed and laughed and laughed. Our parents were downstairs, they thought we were playing nicely in my bedroom . . . but we sneaked into Mom and Dad's room to wrestle on the big bed. It was better for playing on, we had loads of room to fight without falling off and hurting ourselves. And then Maxime farted. We laughed so hard. I tried pushing hard with my tummy like when I poop, and I farted too. I was sitting on the bed and I lifted my butt up a bit to make it louder. Maxime was crying with laughter. And when he calmed down a bit, he explained that what made it so funny was not just the fart, it's that I farted directly on my dad's pillow.

I hadn't even realized, and I began laughing even harder. Just picturing my dad putting his head where I'd farted was the funniest thing ever. And when he saw how funny it was, Maxime took Mom's pillow and farted on that, too.

We kept going for a while, until we couldn't force any more farts out, but we kept giggling for ages, even when we had to go downstairs for dinner. Just seeing Mom and Dad asking us what was so funny, and Auntiphaine and Sylvain saying how silly we were, and looking at us and laughing without knowing what was so funny . . .

Yes, life was better back then. Now everything has changed.

My mom hardly ever laughs these days, and she and Dad are always arguing.

Same for Auntiphaine, but even worse. Mom says she never wants to see her again.

And since no one ever laughs anymore, everyone is watching me all the time. Always asking me questions, spying on me. It makes me so mad!

And I have no one to play with.

So sometimes I think at least Maxime doesn't have to put up with all this. To begin with I thought it was stupid of him to be dead, but now I think maybe it's better not to be here. Not for a long time, just long enough for Mom and Auntiphaine to be friends again. Maybe if I go away for a day or two they will kiss and make up. Because I know they're fighting about me. My mom is mad with Auntiphaine because she thinks I was sick because of her.

But I know that's not true.

What made me sick was eating that funny yellow sugar. I know I shouldn't have done it but I really thought it was brown sugar. I love brown sugar. And there was no one in the kitchen to see what I was up to, so I took a good pinch and tasted it. I did spit most of it out immediately, it was disgusting, but I must have swallowed some.

That's what made me sick. It wasn't Auntiphaine's fault.

So I decided to run away. Just for a day, maybe two. And when I come home, everyone will be friends again and everything will be the same as before.

Maxime will still be gone. I know that.

Mostly *the same as before.*

CHAPTER 50

Milo's attempt to run away rang alarm bells. Not for Laetitia, who had been on high alert for a long time, but for David. He wasn't alarmed about Milo, nor even Tiphaine and Sylvain, but Laetitia. He held her responsible for Milo's little adventure.

Deep down inside, David was torn up with a rage he could barely control. He could not put it into words, but he knew in his heart that Laetitia's suspicions, uncontrollable outbursts, aggressive attitude, and over-the-top reactions were really what had driven Milo to run away. When the police left, the only thing that stopped him from lashing out at her with the full extent of his anger was Milo's presence. He didn't want to sour the atmosphere any further. But one thing he now knew for sure, in his heart and soul: Laetitia was damaging Milo. Badly.

Fury gnawed at him the rest of the day, which he spent with Milo both to give the boy all the comfort and attention he could and to make sure he was not alone with his mother. With a knot in his stomach and a lump in his throat, he avoided her all afternoon and early evening. He was not sure he could hold back his anger if he had to speak to her, and he was unwilling to start yet another fight if he told her what he had really been thinking for several days.

Her idea that Tiphaine was trying to kill Milo was crazy paranoia.

Her suspicions were slowly poisoning his love for her and destroying their family.

And so were her naked scorn for his opinion when it differed from hers and her utter certainty that she was right.

And then there were her misplaced accusations, her ridiculous reactions, the stubborn expression that he sometimes itched to slap off her face. He was fighting a merciless war against the demons of his past that that were urging him to take his revenge.

David was mad at her. He didn't recognize her anymore, he didn't trust her, he no longer understood her. Worse, he had no faith in her. And the thought of leaving Milo alone with her when he went back to work the next day merely strengthened his hostility.

"Are you avoiding me?" she snapped at him. Instinctively, David had recoiled from her as she brushed past him in the kitchen.

His jaw set and teeth clenched, he decided silence was his best course. He rinsed a glass, filled it with orange juice, and turned around to take it upstairs to Milo.

"David, I'm talking to you!" she insisted, her voice harsh, following him. "Are you avoiding me?"

"Leave me alone, Laetitia," he shot back in a hateful whisper.

She gave a short bark of bitter laughter. "You've got to be kidding me!"

He spun around on his heels and interrupted her before she had time to launch into a tirade against injustice and demand his attention, understanding, and support. "No, I'm not kidding! Your son just ran away because his mother is so freaking obsessed with an imaginary threat that she is ready to tear everything down around her!"

"That's not true!" she roared, her face contorted with rage. "You're the one who won't face facts!"

But David refused to listen to her paranoid ramblings anymore. "OK, then, I'm listening!" he bellowed even louder to drown her out. "What is going on, Laetitia? Tell me! Tell me what proof you have, in your twisted mind, that Tiphaine is trying to kill Milo!"

"Not so loud!" she hissed, lowering her own voice. "Milo will hear you!"

"Oh, so *now* you care about what he sees and hears! I mean, it's not like you've been worried about him picking up on your craziness before."

"I'm not crazy, David. It's terrifying that you are still so willfully *blind*."

David's blood boiled as he turned her own words back on her. "What is terrifying, Laetitia, is that you clearly have no idea that your stupid paranoia is destroying our son bit by bit and you are stubbornly clinging to an idea that is completely unfounded. I just can't understand you anymore."

"What do you want me to do, then?" she shot back, getting into her stride. "Am I supposed to just sit around and wait while that bitch tries to get rid of him to say I told you so?"

"I feel sorry for you."

"I don't give a shit about your pity," she screamed. "All I want is for my son to stay safe."

243

Her hysteria just raised a disdainful smile from David. "Look at you," he scoffed. "Freaking nutcase."

Laetitia was so taken aback by his reaction that she was stunned into silence. The two of them heard rustling on the stairs. Turning their heads, they saw Milo, his face etched with misery.

David's heart sank. He had just done to his son exactly what he wanted to avoid. Turning back to Laetitia in a towering rage, he shot her a venomous look. She was gazing at Milo, tears spilling down her cheeks.

"Milo, sweetie . . . ," she said softly, with a sob.

Milo's chin began to quiver and he ran back upstairs to his room. Laetitia made as if to follow him but David grabbed her roughly by the wrist. "Don't you dare go near him!" he spat, barely concealing his loathing.

He let go of her wrist but pinned her with his stare for a few seconds more, ready to grab her again if she made a move. Laetitia stood frozen, an expression of terror on her face, unable to react. David gave her one last threatening look before leaping up the stairs two at a time.

Alone downstairs, Laetitia remained rooted to the spot, flinching only when she heard Milo's bedroom door slamming behind David.

The silence that followed was the final blow.

CHAPTER 51

Daylight was fading but it was still pleasantly warm. If fall had brought a cooler touch to the air, would Laetitia even have felt it? She had left the house robotically, with the crushing sense of being abandoned by her own existence. Rejected by the two people she loved most in the whole world. It's like when you're cast headlong into a nightmare where you're struggling to break free, each passing second a fresh torture. Telling yourself you'll wake up, it must be a dream, life will go back to normal, it has to . . . And then with each passing second, you have to face facts. No. This is your life now. You're not asleep. This is not a nightmare.

It's worse. It's reality.

Panic grips you, and once again, your brain tries to find another way, to return to its regular frequency—the cozy, familiar buzz that up until now has always been there, humming in the background. And soon, despair about not being able to go back in time swallows you up in its infernal maw.

Laetitia kept walking aimlessly. Worn out by a constant sense of unbearable tension, she tried to calm down, hoping that all was not yet lost.

She had never seen David so mad.

He was the man who shielded her from the worries of everyday life. He had never raised his voice. He had been her biggest cheerleader, making things easier for her ever since those terrible early days after her parents died. And now he was the enemy! She needed to keep herself safe from him! The look he had shot her before running upstairs sent a chill down her spine whenever she pictured it.

She had felt like she was in danger.

She knew he was capable of hurting her.

It couldn't be real. It had to be a nightmare.

The thought lessened her sense of horror slightly. But the next second, it came crashing back, plunging its talons into her guts with a cruel twist.

Yet as the minutes passed, step by step, rational thought overcame panic and fear.

Slowly, an alternative story formed in her mind. She clung to it like a life raft in a storm. David's actions were driven by retrospective terror. The pressure had gotten to him and he lost control. He was not himself. Who could blame him? Hadn't she lost it herself, screeching like a demon with Milo just a few steps away? David's reaction was understandable, she could see that now. He didn't really mean what he'd said . . .

Laetitia clung to the thought with the strength of her despair. Once she managed to persuade herself it was just a normal fight—they were both under such pressure—she found herself hoping they could patch things up, praying that David would come around to her point of view. Once the storm of anger had passed, when he sat down to think, to see things her way, everything would go back the way it was.

Her feet had brought her downtown, where the bustling streets were at odds with her somber mood. She had walked aimlessly, driven by her thoughts, and was shocked to find herself so far from home. Now she had found a semblance of inner calm, she was in a hurry to get back, talk things over with David, share her thoughts with him, and maybe even beg for forgiveness.

And to hold Milo tight, kiss his forehead, promise a better and brighter tomorrow . . .

Her watch told her it was now seven. She had been out for almost two hours, and her urgent need to be home put her on edge, heart pounding, mind racing. She thought about hailing a taxi but she had come out without her purse and coat. She had no money and no phone. She couldn't reach David or take the bus, unless she dodged the fare. There was nothing else to do—she would just have to walk. Since she had wandered the streets on the way there, it would probably take her less time to go straight home. An hour's walk, maybe.

Muttering under her breath at her own failings, she set out at a fast clip.

CHAPTER 52

David and Milo were finishing a hastily thrown-together omelet when the doorbell rang.

"Is that Mom?" Milo asked hopefully.

"Probably . . . put the plates in the sink, there's a good boy, and wait for me here."

David wiped his hands on a dishtowel and went to open the door. Torn between the hope of seeing Laetitia safely home and the remnants of his anger, he could not suppress a nervous shiver: what state would he find her in? All he hoped was that she would have calmed down enough not to start fighting again in front of Milo.

Opening the door, he was surprised to see two men on the front step. One asked in an authoritative tone, "David Brunelle?"

Both men were around forty. One wore a corduroy suit, the other a leather jacket. David stared wordlessly at them for a few seconds, his mouth agape. He nodded, frowned, and swallowed painfully. "What is it?" he managed.

"Lieutenant Petraninchi," said the man in the leather jacket, holding up his ID card. "We are investigating the murder of Ernest Wilmot. We need to come inside."

Though Ernest's death had struck David as suspicious, the policeman's words left David dumbstruck. *"Murder?"* he exclaimed in astonishment.

As the two men stepped inside, the second held out a sheet of paper. David took it automatically as he stepped back to let the two men through.

"This is a search warrant for your house. Please let us . . ."

Milo appeared suddenly, putting the man off his stride. The little boy stood in the kitchen doorway, giving the two men a hostile stare.

"Hey there, kiddo," said Lieutenant Petraninchi. "What's your name?"

Milo said nothing. He rushed over to David's side.

"That's right," the other policeman chimed in. "You stay right there with your dad. Everything will be fine." He glanced up at David to make sure he would not cause a scene. The boy being there would make their job easier: everyone would be on their best behavior. The two officers went through to the kitchen.

David followed, Milo close behind him.

The officers conducted a thorough search of the kitchen, inspecting all the cupboards and drawers, emptying the fridge and sniffing the contents of every box and tin. They looked under the sink, poked around in the trash can, and scoured the pantry.

"You and your boy live here alone?"

"No, my wife lives here too."

"Where is she right now?"

"She . . ."

David glanced awkwardly at Milo, clearly wondering how to explain.

"We had an argument," he eventually admitted, opting for the truth. "She went out to clear her head. I . . . I thought you were her when the doorbell rang. I guess she'll be back any minute."

"What were you arguing about?" asked Lieutenant Petraninchi, still searching the kitchen.

Caught off-guard, David paused before answering, "Let's just say we're going through a rough patch."

The officer gave David an appraising stare, looked down at Milo, and nodded understandingly. They went through to the living room and began searching.

"What are you looking for exactly?" David asked after a while. No reply.

"Is there an outside light for the yard?" asked Lieutenant Petraninchi.

David flicked the switch, lighting up the terrace as Petraninchi slid the French windows open and took a few steps outside. His colleague set about searching the dining room. Both men were perfectly methodical, calm and unhurried.

Milo and David stayed in the living room. David watched as Petraninchi unhooked a flashlight from his belt and strode toward the end of the yard, sweeping the grass and shrubs with its beam.

Now they were alone in the room, Milo whispered, "Dad, what are the police doing here?"

"Nothing to worry about, son. Everything's fine."

"When will Mom be back?"

"Soon."

David wanted to do more to reassure Milo, but anxiety knotted his own guts and it was taking all he had to maintain an outwardly calm appearance. His mind raced with a million questions, but the fear of betraying his nerves froze all rational thought. What did Ernest really die of? Why the search? Why at his house? Was he on the list of suspects? Was his criminal past finally catching up with him? Or was this normal procedure, since he was one of the last people to see Ernest alive? But then why not summon him to the police station, like the day after Ernest died? Were the officers looking for something specific? Did they think they had some evidence? Or was this just a stab in the dark?

David's thoughts were soon interrupted by Petraninchi calling from the terrace:

"Bonaud! Come and see this!"

The other officer came in from the dining room and went out to join Petraninchi. David's heart started pounding. What had he found? He stepped out onto the terrace after Bonaud, ordering Milo to wait inside. But the boy wouldn't listen. He began to follow David out, forcing him to turn back.

"Wait here, Milo, I'll be back in just a second!"

"Don't leave me here by myself, Daddy!"

The little boy's terrified plea broke David's heart. He stayed with Milo, craning his neck to peer out at the terrace. A few seconds later, Petraninchi and Bonaud reappeared.

"What's going on?" David asked, failing to quell the tremor in his voice.

"Everything's fine, sir."

Seeming to consider the issue closed, they carried on with the search, going through the rooms upstairs, the cellar, and even David's taxi with a fine-toothed comb. It was a good twenty minutes before Lieutenant Petraninchi took him to one side.

"You need to come with us to the station, Mr. Brunelle. We have a few questions for you."

"But I told your colleague everything, the day after Ernest died . . . ," David protested feebly.

Petraninchi gave him an insistent, slightly threatening stare. "Sir . . . don't make me cuff you in front of your son," he murmured. "Can you ask someone to look after him until your wife gets back?"

Panicking at the unexpected turn of events, David shook his head, unable to get his thoughts in order.

"In that case, we'll have to bring him, too," the officer continued, "but I really don't think that's the best idea, for him or for you. Is there really no one you can ask?"

"No . . ."

"No family, no friends, no neighbors?"

Neighbors . . . David swallowed painfully, his mouth dry. Of course, he could ask Tiphaine and Sylvain, but was that a good idea given the circumstances? Time was of the essence. Petraninchi was still staring at him, making it hard to think rationally.

No, not Tiphaine and Sylvain. Laetitia would never forgive him.

Or he could take Milo with him to the police station and have him wait in one of those chilly, impersonal, hostile rooms . . . a terrifying experience for a seven-year-old who knew his father was being held for questioning on the other side of the wall. Sordid memories from David's teenage years came rushing back—the hours of questioning, policemen playing mind games, fear, doubt, hatred . . . and sometimes violence . . . the images jostled in his mind with sounds and smells he had hoped never to encounter again, even in his worst nightmares.

David knew there was no way he could subject his son to that. He would not have the strength to face the police with his precious boy just a few steps away, behind a locked door. Milo was his Achilles heel: the boy's mere presence made him vulnerable. If he wanted to keep his wits about him, he had to keep his boy safe. Better to choose the lesser evil.

"I'll ask the neighbors," he muttered.

"OK, then, let's go."

David numbly approached Milo, knelt down, and explained what was happening.

"Listen, sweetie, I need to go with these policemen. It won't take long, I'll be back soon. I'll take you around to Auntiphaine's, she can look after you until Mom gets back. OK?"

"I want to stay with you, Daddy," begged Milo, his voice quavering.

"You can't, I'm afraid, sweetheart . . . it's not a place for little boys . . . you'll be better off with Auntiphaine."

Milo looked down at his shoes, tears rolling down his cheeks. David felt his heart snap in two. He hugged the boy tight.

"We need to go now, Mr. Brunelle," insisted Bonaud, just behind him.

David stood up and took Milo's hand.

Then he took him to ring Tiphaine and Sylvain's bell.

Opening the door, Tiphaine could not hide her astonishment. Finding David on her doorstep with Milo and two stony-faced strangers left her speechless.

"I don't have time to explain," began David before she could find her voice. "I have to go out for the evening and Laetitia has gone out for a walk. She'll be back soon. At least, I hope so. Can you look after Milo?"

"Of course."

Sylvain appeared behind Tiphaine. David acknowledged him with a brief nod, then spoke again after a moment's hesitation. "To be honest, Laetitia and I had an argument. She stormed out. I don't know when she'll be back. And she doesn't know what's going on here."

"Is everything OK, David?" asked Tiphaine, staring at the two men behind him.

"Yes . . . it's about Ernest's death. Nothing serious. I'll be home later tonight. First thing in the morning at the latest."

Milo was clinging to his hand. David held his arm out toward Tiphaine, forcing the boy to step forward. Tiphaine welcomed the little boy with obvious affection.

David cast one last glance at his son and forced himself to smile. A smile of unfathomable sadness. As he left, he held out the house keys to Tiphaine.

"Like I said, Laetitia stormed out. She forgot her keys. Can you keep an eye out for her, or put a note on the door to tell her I'm leaving you the keys and Milo is with you?"

"I doubt she'll be very happy . . ."

"You're the only solution."

He turned and walked down the street to the police car, flanked by the two officers.

Tiphaine watched from the doorstep until the car turned the corner. Then she looked down at Milo and tenderly stroked his hair. "Come on inside, Milo, you'll catch cold. Have you eaten?"

He nodded. Tiphaine closed the door behind her.

"Let's get you ready for bed, then . . . Go and wait for me upstairs, I'll be up in a moment. You can choose a book if you'd like to read a story."

Milo began to climb the stairs slowly.

Tiphaine and Sylvain exchanged stunned, victorious glances.

"It's now or never!" she whispered as soon as Milo was out of earshot. "We'll never get another chance like this!"

Laetitia got home twenty minutes later. No keys. She rang the bell.

No one came to the door.

CHAPTER 53

"David! Please! Open the door! We need to talk . . ."

Laetitia pulled on the door handle for the tenth time in a row, knowing it was pointless. The door would not open. She rang the bell over and over, then banged on the wood. David seemed deaf to her entreaties. Was he so mad he would leave her on the doorstep all night? She couldn't believe it. Whatever he had against her, he couldn't stop her from entering her own house!

Staggered at a vengefulness that was not like the David she knew, Laetitia soon gave up banging on the door. Sunset had brought a chill in the air and she began to shiver with cold and panic.

What was going on?

How had it come to this?

Since Maxime's death, her life had collapsed around her into a never-ending nightmare. As if the little boy's fall had dragged down her entire world, the life she had been living contentedly for so many years. Losing Tiphaine and Sylvain as friends had already struck a blow to her happiness, which seemed increasingly fragile. But without David, without *Milo*, she was nothing.

Crazed with fear at a situation that had spun out of her

control, Laetitia felt panic gripping her gut. She began to sob openly outside the stubbornly locked door. "David, please! I'm begging you, open up!"

The silence inside the house devastated her. It was not their first argument, and even though this fight had struck deeper and harder than the others, that was no reason to ignore her completely.

With a superhuman effort, Laetitia choked down her tears and went around to the dining room window. She put her nose to the pane, shielding her eyes with her hands to peer through the sheer curtain. No movement. No lights. That was normal: they often ate in the kitchen at the back of the house when they were alone. But if David was in the kitchen, she should have been able to see a dim ring of light around the dining room door . . .

Clearly, there was no one downstairs.

A faint hope rose in her chest. She'd found an explanation for David's prolonged silence. He must be in the bathroom, maybe even in the shower. He couldn't hear her ringing the bell or banging on the door, let alone shouting.

She took a few steps back and looked up at the top floor. The bathroom was on the right, overlooking the street. The window was dark. It looked as empty as the ground floor.

Maybe David was in Milo's room, putting the little boy to bed, or in their own room? Wherever he was in the house, he should be able to hear her!

Laetitia plunged back into the depths of despair. There was only one reason David wasn't opening the door: he wanted her out.

Alone in the night, clad in just a thin sweater and light pants that did little to keep out the chilly fall air, with no ID, cash, or credit card, Laetitia felt at an utter loss. She went back to the front door and slumped to the floor, giving free rein to a rising tide of panic. Everyone she had ever loved had abandoned her, scorned and rejected her. She huddled up, knees to her chest, and burst into tears.

"Laetitia? What are you doing there?"

The unexpected voice startled her. Looking up, through her tears she saw the blurred figure of Tiphaine approaching. Her neighbor knelt beside her at a careful distance, asking, "Did you forget your keys?"

Too worn out from a tidal wave of emotions to reject the woman she considered her worst enemy, Laetitia just shook her head.

"You must be freezing!" Tiphaine continued sympathetically. "How could David have gone out leaving you like this?"

Laetitia immediately stopped sobbing. She looked up and stared at Tiphaine in shock. "David's gone?" she managed to murmur, her voice trembling.

"Yes," Tiphaine replied. "I thought you knew. They left a good hour ago, maybe even longer . . ."

"He . . . he took Milo?"

Tiphaine looked surprised. "Laetitia, what's going on? I saw David put Milo in his taxi with two suitcases in the trunk. I thought . . . I was sure you were all going somewhere, probably because of me . . . you wanted to get away . . . looks like I was wrong!"

Even worse than David's stubborn refusal to open the door,

the thought that he had left her, taking their son away, was the final crushing blow to Laetitia. A low moan of pain escaped her as she felt her heart explode in her chest. If David was furious enough to take her son away from her, then all was lost.

"You can't stay here, Laetitia. You'll die of cold!" Tiphaine continued, her voice oozing with what sounded like concern.

Die of cold? What did it matter now?

"Come on!" Tiphaine implored, maintaining her kindly tone. "You can warm up at our place. Then if the French windows aren't locked you can get in through the yard."

Laetitia did not react. David had left. Milo was gone. Nothing else mattered.

Seeing Laetitia inert on the doorstep, Tiphaine tried to help her stand. She put one arm around Laetitia and heaved her up, leaning on the door for support. Laetitia slumped against her like a deadweight. Once the pair were standing, Tiphaine slipped her other arm around Laetitia's waist and half carried, half dragged her next door.

As soon as they were inside, Tiphaine pushed the door shut with her foot.

It shut with a sinister slam.

A few minutes later, the telephone rang in Laetitia and David's living room. The answering machine switched on after five rings and Milo's voice echoed through the empty room.

"You've reached the Brunelles. We are out right now but please leave a message after the beep."

The incandescent voice of Roger Forton, David's boss at the taxi company, filled the air.

"Brunelle, Roger Forton here! What the hell do you think you're playing at? Who do you take yourself for? I just got a call from an attorney. It seems you dragged a client out of the taxi while you were on a job and dumped him on the sidewalk. He's planning to sue! So listen here, Brunelle. I'm prepared to hear your side of the story but I warn you, if you did kick the guy out of your taxi before he got where he wanted to go, you are out of a job! I won't put up with lazy scumbags on my watch. You'd better get back to me soon!"

CHAPTER 54

As soon as David arrived at the police station, an officer took his fingerprints and read him his rights. He was then taken to an interview room to be questioned about his relationship with Ernest. Having some experience with police investigations, he kept his cool and answered every question as plainly and simply as he could. On the way to the station he had tried to get a grip and analyze the situation. He had nothing to do with Ernest's death, directly or indirectly, so he had nothing to fear. That was all that mattered.

From the line of questioning, he quickly grasped that his old friend's heart attack was triggered by poisoning. Laetitia was right: Ernest's death was anything but natural.

The police were obviously on the hunt for a motive, which was what brought them to his past connection with Ernest. His criminal past would be a black mark against him, for sure. But what had David really worried was the sense of quiet certainty he could feel around him. They were sure they had solid proof incriminating him in some way or another.

It had to be a bluff, he thought. He was sure there were no illicit substances of any kind in his house, let alone poison strong enough to trigger a heart attack.

"You nearly got away with it!" said Lieutenant Bonaud forcefully. "Forensics nearly missed it. What you didn't know was that whatever shit it was you fed him brought on kidney failure, and that didn't fit with the diagnosis. Wow, better luck next time, huh!"

Realizing the interview was spiraling beyond his control, David requested an attorney. He knew that anything he said could be taken down in evidence and used against him in a court of law. Not knowing exactly what was going on, he might say something that could prove harmful to his defense.

He didn't have an attorney, so the police called a court-appointed lawyer. David was locked in a cell to wait.

Alone in the cell, he had plenty of time to quell a rising wave of panic and think about what lay ahead. The cops had plenty of questions, but so did he. Who would gain by killing Ernest? His old friend was getting old, he'd been retired for years, and he'd never mentioned any dispute with any of the ex-prisoners he'd supervised at work. Admittedly, Ernest was not one to divulge his innermost thoughts, and it was not in his nature to share concerns, even if he felt he might be in danger. But why had the cops come knocking on *his* door? Was it just because his old friend had spent the afternoon at his house, or was there more to it? Was there some mysterious evidence pointing a finger at him?

What you didn't know was that whatever shit it was you fed him brought on kidney failure, and that didn't fit with the diagnosis.

He deduced that Ernest had consumed some deadly poison. He had not been spiked with a needle during an assault. But what poison could cause a heart attack *and* kidney failure? How could the police have found evidence at his house, when all he had were a few ordinary household medicines, none of which could possibly kill anyone as far as he knew? Every question came to a dead end.

Turning all these questions over in his mind, he felt his sense of calm slip away little by little. He wished he could talk to Laetitia, let her know what was happening, pass on the few snippets of information he'd picked up and ask her to look them up online to find out more. Maybe if he found out what the poison was, he could figure out who Ernest's killer might be.

The cell door swung open, interrupting his thoughts. A young man in a gray suit over a white shirt with the top button undone and no tie came in and introduced himself. "I'm Gérard Depardieu. You can call me Mr. Depardieu. I've been appointed as your lawyer."

"Is this some kind of joke?" asked David, chuckling a little, though he knew it was no laughing matter.

"Yes, that is my real name," the attorney replied wearily. He'd clearly heard it all before. "Let's get down to business, if that's OK with you. My name might sound like a joke, but I promise you I'm effective in a courtroom. None of my clients have ever complained."

He was on the young side, David thought, but the attorney's quick wit and air of quiet confidence put him somewhat at ease.

"We have half an hour to talk alone before the police take you back in for further questioning. I've had a quick look through your file," the attorney continued, not wasting a second. David was impressed with his efficiency. "I need to hear your version of events. I'll tell you now that the evidence against you is thin to nonexistent. I thought it was a joke at first. They've been laying it on thick in the hope of getting you to crack under pressure. You'll be back home within an hour."

"What's the evidence?"

Mr. Depardieu gave a small, sly smile.

"You have foxgloves growing in a pot on your terrace."

"*What?*"

"The autopsy found traces of digitoxin in the victim's body."

"Digitoxin?"

"It's a powerful phytosteroid extracted from foxgloves, some impressive specimens of which are growing on your terrace. They act as a diuretic, leading to increased urine output. The pathologist's report states that the form of digitoxin found in the victim's urine is pure enough to indicate direct ingestion of the plant itself."

"Absolute bullshit!"

"I'm with you there . . . was he vegetarian?"

"I beg your pardon?"

"Sorry. Bad joke."

David was impervious to the attorney's ill-timed humor. As the realization hit him that Ernest had been poisoned by a plant, his blood froze in his veins and his hair stood up on his neck. Foxgloves . . . that rang a vague bell. Searching his memory, he felt the ground give way beneath his feet. Tiphaine at the door, clutching a plant pot full of pretty purple bell-shaped blooms in one hand and a beautifully wrapped present in the other.

And this is for Laetitia. It's a foxglove. She can plant it in the yard or leave it in its pot on the terrace, either is fine. It was being thrown out at work and my yard is already full. It's pretty and it flowers all summer.

Tiphaine had literally planted evidence of their guilt in their yard.

He knew only one person capable of using pretty flowers as a deadly weapon.

And he had entrusted his son to her an hour before.

CHAPTER 55

Huddled on Tiphaine and Sylvain's sofa, Laetitia sobbed on and on, unable to master her emotions.

How could David do such a thing? Where had he taken Milo?

What was he planning?

How could she carry on if she lost her husband and son for good?

Each minute that passed without answers seemed an insurmountable ordeal, worse still when she realized it was unlikely she would hear from them overnight. If David had seen her absence as a chance to get away, he wasn't going to get back in touch barely two hours after leaving her.

And now she was with Tiphaine and Sylvain, the point of origin of her journey to hell. Tiphaine had sat down by her side, trying to soothe her with soft, hopeful words. *"They'll be back, don't worry. People sometimes do crazy things when they're mad—you know that as well as I do. Things will look brighter in the morning. I'm sure they'll be back home tomorrow. You can sleep here, if you like."*

Sleep here? But where?

In Maxime's bed? Never!

And then other images began to flit through Laetitia's mind. Her own bed, cold and unwelcoming without David. Milo's empty room in a deserted house. A night that would never end.

Laetitia knew she would never have the strength to go back home tonight. She would never find the courage to face up to Milo and David's absence. She stopped resisting, not caring about her own fate.

"I'll make you herbal tea to help you sleep."

Just as Tiphaine got up to head for the kitchen, Sylvain appeared in the doorway. Tiphaine wordlessly questioned him with an insistent gaze. He nodded almost imperceptibly and followed her into the kitchen.

"What are you up to?" he asked nervously as soon as they were out of earshot.

"What we planned."

Sylvain stiffened, chewing his lower lip, ill at ease. Taking no note of Sylvain's anxiety, Tiphaine bustled around the kitchen, putting the kettle on to boil and fetching a mug and the packet of herbal tea. She took an infuser from the drawer and filled it generously with a restful blend of mint, linden blossom, and verbena. Sylvain watched nervously without moving a muscle.

Then Tiphaine opened another drawer and took out an unlabeled bottle of Lexotan. She popped it open and took out three tablets. She started to put the lid back on, hesitated, and then took out a fourth.

"Go and see what's she's doing!" she ordered Sylvain, irritated by his still, watchful presence.

"Tiphaine . . ."

"Go and sit with her!"

He sighed and did as she asked. Just before he left the kitchen, she snapped, "Now is not the time to go soft on me, Sylvain!"

He turned and looked at her solemnly.

"Right?" she insisted, her voice sharp.

"Don't worry."

Then he went and joined Laetitia in the living room.

Alone in the kitchen, Tiphaine set about grinding the four Lexotan tablets to a fine powder, which she poured into the mug. The kettle was whistling, so she grabbed a potholder and carefully added the boiling water. The Lexotan powder dissolved instantly. She placed the tea infuser in the mug and left it to steep for a few minutes. Standing in the silent kitchen, she smiled. Not evilly, or even triumphantly. Serenely.

After five minutes, she removed the infuser.

Two sugars.

There. Ready.

Back in the living room, she found Sylvain sitting on the sofa by Laetitia's side, in the spot she had vacated. Laetitia had stopped crying and was staring into space, her eyes red and ringed with dark smudges. No one spoke. Sylvain was looking down at his feet, occasionally glancing up at Laetitia, a slight air of bewilderment on his face. She seemed oblivious.

For a second or two, Tiphaine thought that Sylvain might

have talked to Laetitia. Fear rose in her throat. She hurried over, hoping to catch Sylvain's attention. He looked up, and their eyes met.

She read in his gaze that their secret was safe. He would follow her to the bitter end.

"Come on, Laetitia, drink this. It will help you sleep."

Laetitia started in surprise, seeming to return to earth with a jolt as Tiphaine knelt down to hand her a steaming mug.

"What is it?" asked Laetitia, her voice hoarse, almost dazed.

"A nice warm drink. Mint, linden blossom, verbena. It'll do you good."

Laetitia raised the mug to her lips and took a tiny sip. She made as if to put it down, but Tiphaine gestured to her to drink up.

Laetitia meekly obeyed, indifferent to her surroundings. She took another sip, larger this time, and then a third, encouraged by Tiphaine, who gently but firmly urged her to finish it all.

"Drink it all up," she soothed. "You'll feel much better."

Laetitia drained the mug to the very last drop.

She saw Tiphaine's face looming over her, smiling kindly. She watched her take the empty mug from her hands and place it carefully on the coffee table, next to a booklet. A child's medical records. The name Maxime Geniot on the cover.

Memories of the little boy clamped over her chest like a vise. She would never again hug him tight, never hear his giggles, never watch over him as he slept. She thought the pain would smother her. Then for one long-drawn-out second that seemed to last an eternity, Milo's and Maxime's faces merged in the blur of her tears. She thought briefly her mind was playing tricks on her. Her eyelids grew impossibly heavy.

Within a few minutes, she was lost in deep, dreamless sleep.

When Tiphaine was confident Laetitia was completely out, she headed back into the kitchen, returning moments later with unlabeled bottles of pills—Ambien, Xanax, Effexor—and a Tupperware full of a gray powder of her own making. A blend she knew would leave Laetitia no chance of survival.

"Come and help me," she asked Sylvain.

He was still sitting by Laetitia, keeping watch. He helped her peel the little foil packets open one by one. Tiphaine gathered up the pills and crushed them, adding a handful of Reglan to prevent vomiting.

"Bring me the bottle of whiskey."

Sylvain did as he was asked. Tiphaine poured the amber liquid into a glass, added the crushed pills and some powder from the Tupperware, and gave it a good stir.

"Sit her up."

Her voice was taut with concentration, but she spoke without violence or aggression. Sylvain put his arm around Laetitia's shoulders as she lay slumped on the sofa and pulled her into a sitting position.

Tiphaine sat down by her.

With infinite care, she trickled the lethal mixture down Laetitia's throat with slow, methodical gestures, tipping her head back each time to dribble the liquid down her throat.

When the glass was empty, Tiphaine and Sylvain gazed at Laetitia's inert body with watchful eyes. She seemed to be fast asleep, her face scarily pale and covered in a thin film of sweat that highlighted her bloodless complexion.

Gradually, her respiration became irregular, her chest heaving in ragged puffs. The gaps between breaths grew longer as the seconds ticked by.

After twenty minutes, Laetitia sighed one last, soft breath.

CHAPTER 56

Panicking at the terrifying implications of his sudden realization, David begged his attorney to get him out of the police station. He had to get home and pick his son up right away. Mr. Depardieu tried to make sense of his story, his head whirling as his client shouted he was innocent and accused his neighbor—the same one who had taken in his son a short while before.

"But why did you hand your son over if you thought she was a potential killer?"

"I didn't know Ernest had been poisoned!"

"What does that change?"

"Tiphaine is an expert herbalist! She can make concoctions that would kill an elephant in a matter of minutes . . ." David gave a brief account of the episode ten days earlier that had nearly cost Milo his life.

"Wait . . . did your son eat something he wasn't supposed to, or did your neighbor try and poison him deliberately?"

"My wife thinks she tried to kill him."

"What do you think?"

"I thought she was making it up. But now, with this digitoxin business, I . . ."

"OK. Let's say she did. But let me ask you one simple question: what possible reason could she have for killing Ernest Wilmot?"

David had no answer to that. He sat in silence for a full minute, trying to come up with a potential motive.

"No idea," he eventually had to admit. "But what I do know is I have to get out of here. Now."

"I'm on it."

Depardieu rose to his feet and banged on the cell door. He told the guard that his client wanted to get the questioning over and done with. They were taken to an interrogation room to wait for a few moments before Petraninchi and Bonaud joined them.

Mr. Depardieu was right. There was simply not enough evidence to keep David in any longer. The presence of the poisonous foxgloves on his terrace was hardly proof.

Forty-five minutes later, David was out of the police station and on his way home at top speed.

CHAPTER 57

Tiphaine and Sylvain had no difficulty transporting Laetitia back to her own living room. She was almost small and light enough for Sylvain to carry her alone. The only trouble was getting her over the hedge between the two yards: it was much too risky to take her out on the street, where any of the neighbors might spot them.

Tiphaine went first. She stood on a chair, threw one leg over the branches and dropped down on the other side, soft as a cat. Sylvain hoisted Laetitia over the hedge, where Tiphaine caught the body as it came down. Not a scratch. Then Sylvain clambered over.

As they had hoped, the French windows in the living room were unlocked. It hardly mattered, since David had given them the keys.

Once inside, they discussed where to leave the body.

Tiphaine thought the sofa was the most obvious spot.

Sylvain agreed. He carefully placed Laetitia down, stretching her out on the cushions while Tiphaine arranged the barbiturates and empty whisky bottle on the sofa next to her.

They stood silently for a few seconds, breathing heavily as

they surveyed the scene, looking out for clues that might betray them. Or at least run counter to the suicide scenario.

"Wait!" Tiphaine suddenly exclaimed.

"What?"

"I'll be right back!"

She dashed back outside and climbed over the hedge. She was back in a minute or two, clutching her purse.

"What are you doing?" asked Sylvain, nervous yet intrigued.

She wordlessly opened her pocketbook and handed her husband a sheet of paper folded in two. He opened it to read two simple words in Laetitia's handwriting:

Forgive me.

"What's this?" he asked in surprise.

"A note she wrote me a while back."

"What did she want you to forgive?"

"I'll tell you later. We need to get out of here. David could be back any minute."

She put the note in plain sight on the coffee table by the sofa and glanced around the room once more. Then the pair left the house, carefully closing the French windows behind them.

CHAPTER 58

Tiphaine was right. No sooner were they back home than David was ringing the bell and thumping on their door. Slightly panicked at the speed of events, Tiphaine nonetheless took the time to dip a wad of cotton wool in a powerful soporific—another of her concoctions—and hand it to Sylvain as she headed for the door.

"You need to jump him as soon as he sets foot inside," she whispered. "We need to take him by surprise, or we'll never manage."

"Yeah, I know what I'm doing."

Sylvain hid behind the door. When it opened, he would be out of sight. They exchanged one last glance, making sure they were ready, then Tiphaine threw open the door.

Before she could open her mouth to speak, David hurled himself at her, grabbing her collar and slamming her against the hallway wall. He held her there, his surprise attack letting him put her in a headlock and begin squeezing. All Tiphaine could do was claw at his forearm as she struggled for air.

"Where's Milo?" he spat, his face a few inches from hers.

Unable to speak, Tiphaine wriggled as hard as she could to escape. He loosened his grip for an instant to let her talk.

"David, what's got into you?"

"WHERE IS MILO?" he roared, losing his last shred of self-control.

"Upstairs! He's asleep!" she managed to choke the words out.

David began to apply more pressure, staring straight into Tiphaine's eyes with a gaze full of hatred.

"Listen to me, you bitch, I don't know exactly what you did to Ernest or why, but I know you killed him. So now . . ."

Before he could get the rest of the sentence out, Sylvain stepped out silently from behind the door. He grabbed the back of David's neck tight and held the wad of cotton wool over his nose. David let go of Tiphaine in surprise and wheeled around suddenly, trying to knock Sylvain off his feet. Sylvain staggered but held on, clinging to David's shoulders. Furious at having fallen for such an obvious ruse, David kicked and struggled like a wounded bull, throwing Sylvain back against the wall. With each kick, Sylvain was crushed under David's full weight, but he held on.

Tiphaine recovered quickly from David's attack and looked on in horror at the two men locked together in struggle. She was briefly tempted to fetch a heavy object to knock David out, but a blow to the head would ruin their entire plan. There must be no trace of a physical assault.

Finally, Tiphaine's concoction began to take effect. David's jerks and twists grew feebler, and soon he was stumbling around, unable to fight on. Seeing victory in his grasp, Sylvain clamped the wad tighter over his nose.

After a long minute, David collapsed to the floor, pinning Sylvain under him.

Tiphaine rushed over to free her husband. He had softened David's fall. "Are you OK?"

Sylvain nodded, catching his breath as he gathered his composure. "He nearly screwed up the whole plan."

"Let's get a move on. We need to get him back home."

It proved much harder to get David over the hedge than Laetitia. At one point, Tiphaine was tempted to take him through the front door instead. But it was too risky. She and Sylvain could keep watch for anyone coming in the street, but they could not be sure none of the other neighbors were watching from a window. Damn neighbors! Tiphaine regretfully conceded they had no choice. She wasn't strong enough to catch David's deadweight as Sylvain lowered him over the hedge. But if Sylvain just dropped him over, he would fall to the terrace and develop suspicious bruising.

"We need something to break his fall," Sylvain pointed out. "We can hoist him to the top of the hedge together, then drop him on the other side."

"A mattress!"

This turned out to be an effective solution.

Then they had to get David upstairs into his own bedroom, past Laetitia's body on the sofa, the pills scattered across the floor, the note still on the table. Once they were in the hallway, Sylvain took David by the shoulders while Tiphaine held his feet.

It was hard going, but they made it upstairs. While Sylvain went back home for a rope, Tiphaine caught her breath. She sneaked back downstairs to put David's keys on the table in the hall.

When Sylvain was back, they knotted the rope solidly around the top of the banisters on the upstairs landing, then fashioned a noose to slip around David's neck.

And finally, with the last of their strength, they hoisted his inert body up onto the banister and toppled it over.

CHAPTER 59

"Wake up, Milo. Time to get ready for school . . ."

The little boy's eyelashes fluttered as he blinked awake. He yawned and stretched, then swung his feet out of bed.

"Did you sleep well?"

Milo nodded.

"What would you like for breakfast?"

"Crepes!"

Tiphaine smiled. "Crepes it is! Do you need help putting your clothes on?"

"I can get dressed by myself!" he protested, his voice heavy with sleep.

"I'm sure you can, sweetie. Come on, up and at 'em. I'll wait for you downstairs."

She headed for the door.

"Where are Mom and Dad?" Milo asked, the memory of the evening's events coming back to him.

Tiphaine turned to him with a reassuring smile.

"They're not back yet . . . but don't worry. I'm sure they'll be home soon."

Milo's face darkened, bringing Tiphaine back to his side.

"What's up, sweetie?" she asked, gently stroking his hair.

"I want my mom and dad . . ."

"I know, Milo . . . listen, here's the plan. You get your clothes on while I make some crepes, I'll take you to school, and I'm sure at the end of the day, your mom will come and pick you up. How does that sound?"

That brought an instant smile to Milo's face.

"And you like it here, with Auntiphaine and Sylvain, don't you?"

"Yeah!"

She gave the little boy a bear hug. "Everything will be fine, you'll see," she murmured, smothering him with kisses.

A few minutes later she found Sylvain making coffee in the kitchen. Immediately he asked how Milo was feeling.

"He slept well," Tiphaine assured him.

"Did he ask for his parents?"

"Of course. It's only natural. But he'll get used to it soon enough."

She went over to Sylvain, who had his back to her, and snuggled into him with a sigh of happiness.

"We're so nearly there . . . just one more step. But the worst of it is behind us. It'll all go back to the way it was before." With a bright smile, she added, "I told you the chance would come . . . we just had to be patient!"

Sylvain turned around and hugged her.

"It's true, you were right. As usual. But I still think there was no need to kill Ernest," he said, with a hint of reproach.

"That's not true! Ernest was Milo's godfather. If he'd wanted to adopt the boy, we would have been in trouble."

"Ernest would never have done that. He hated kids!"

"Not Milo. He loved Milo. And I didn't want to take the risk."

It had been perfectly straightforward. When she spied Ernest leaving Milo's birthday party, she went out to talk to him, then invited him in for coffee, claiming she had something to discuss. The digitoxin she stirred into the old man's coffee did the rest for her.

"Being Milo's godmother doesn't automatically mean he comes to you," Sylvain objected.

"I know. But we are all he has. Everyone will back us up on that."

"People will know we weren't on the best of terms recently . . ."

"People think the four of us were joined at the hip. Around the neighborhood, at school, everyone knows we were best friends. All friends fall out occasionally. And everyone will see it as the obvious solution. The judge, social services. And we'll fight for it, right?"

Sylvain gazed at her anxiously, saying nothing. Tiphaine asked again, a sharp edge to her words, "We'll fight for it, right? We'll fight for Milo, for us, to be a proper family again."

"Yes, sweetheart," he murmured after a pause, kissing her softly on the forehead.

Then he gently broke free from her embrace to spoon the coffee into the machine filter.

"What time are you planning to call the police?" he asked as he hit the on button.

"Around lunchtime."

"You think they'll buy the suicide scenario?"

Tiphaine pursed her lips and shrugged as if to say it was a no-brainer.

"I can't see what other conclusions they could come to . . ."

Sylvain opened the top cupboard and brought out three plates and three cups.

"Maybe we should have tried some of your fairy dust again."

"Too risky," retorted Tiphaine, taking the milk from the fridge and placing it on the table. "You saw what happened last time. Milo could have died!"

She shivered at the thought of the tragedy that would have occurred if Milo had died from the poison she had prepared for David and Laetitia. A blend of the most powerfully toxic medicinal plants in her yard. How careless of her to leave the bowl within his reach! Trying to be efficient, she had prepped the poison in advance, then left it on the side so it would be there when she needed it. It hardly mattered if David or Laetitia noticed the bowl: there were always random pots and dishes full of mysterious powders, dried leaves, herbal teas, bark, plant extracts, and other concoctions sitting around in Tiphaine's kitchen.

Sylvain put a knife alongside each plate.

"You're right," he agreed. "I just hope there's no problem with the suicide story."

"Trust me. I thought of everything."

Sylvain ran an eye over the kitchen table. Everything was

in its rightful place. He pointed out, "No such thing as the perfect murder."

Ah, he'd forgotten the bread.

"Well, let's say we just proved that wrong," Tiphaine declared, putting a baguette down in the middle of the table.

She turned around, opened the fridge, and sighed. "Where *did* I put that crepe batter?"

CHAPTER 60

Tiphaine called the police at around noon.

She hadn't seen or heard her neighbors since the day before. They were very close friends who had left their child with her overnight. She was worried. The couple had been going through a rough patch, constantly fighting; she often heard them screaming at each other through the wall. Yesterday, after the umpteenth blazing row, Laetitia had left, slamming the door. Her friend had been depressed for a number of weeks, which made her prone to overreacting and paranoia. Her husband was finding her increasingly hard to deal with. Just yesterday, her constant ranting and raving had driven their seven-year-old to run away from home. Lieutenant Chapuy and Lieutenant Delaunoy would confirm that Laetitia's mental health was fragile and that the couple was on the verge of splitting. When the child was found wandering the streets, the argument had gotten out of hand, both parents blaming each other, and Laetitia had stormed out. The problem was that later that evening, two other policemen had come to their house about the death of another friend of theirs, and David had had to accompany them to the station. He had left their son, Milo, with her, giving her his keys in case Laetitia came home.

Laetitia had returned at about half past eight. Finding the door locked, she had naturally rung the bell next door. Tiphaine had opened it to find her friend in a pitiful state, eyes red with weeping, exhaustion etched on her face, her mood the blackest she had ever seen. Tiphaine told her two police officers had taken David away, something to do with Ernest's death. The news had sent Laetitia into a tailspin: she demanded David's keys. Tiphaine handed them over, reassuring her that Milo was safely tucked up in bed upstairs. Laetitia preferred to leave him sleeping.

Then she went home . . .

And that was the last she had heard. No word from Laetitia, or from David.

The policeman told Tiphaine over the phone that David and Laetitia were adults and, as such, were free to come and go as they pleased. It had only been a few hours, far too soon to worry.

Tiphaine pointed out that they had agreed that one of them would pick the boy up in the morning to take him to school. David's taxi was still parked down the street, and when she rang the bell, no one answered the door. Neither was picking up the land line or answering their cell phone. If the police officer couldn't help her, could he at least check whether David was still at the station? If not, at what time exactly did he leave?

He put her on hold for a minute or two.

Then he came back on the line, telling her David had left the station late last evening.

Tiphaine feigned further concern. Why hadn't he come by when the police let him go, as he had promised? And why had neither parent come to pick their son up that morning?

The policeman informed her that if she wanted to report a missing person, she would have to come down to the station herself. Tiphaine thanked him, hung up, and got ready to head out. The quicker the case was opened, the quicker they could draw a line under it all and get on with their lives.

The mysterious disappearance of a couple who were supposed to pick up their child raised red flags at the station. And they were even more inclined to act when Chapuy and Delaunoy confirmed Laetitia's vulnerable mental state. A team of two officers set out with Tiphaine to inspect David and Laetitia's house.

Was Tiphaine sure she saw Laetitia entering the house last night?

Tiphaine repeated her statement without a second's hesitation. The last time she saw her neighbor, she was on her own doorstep, watching Laetitia slip the key in the lock and step into her front hall.

After knocking and ringing the bell to no avail, the officers decided to call a locksmith. Some minutes later, they were inside.

The suicide theory was rapidly confirmed. When the news was radioed back to the station, Bonaud and Petraninchi took it as a confession of David Brunelle's culpability in the death of Ernest Wilmot.

Was Laetitia Brunelle an accomplice or an unwitting participant, they wondered? Either way, she clearly couldn't bear the burden of guilt—her own or her husband's. When she got home, upon learning that he had been taken in for questioning, her depression had got the best of her. She must have given in to panic before taking her own life. The note in her own hand on the table by her body proved it.

Then when David got home in turn, his world collapsed. He must have found his wife's body, the note begging for forgiveness, the pills strewn on the carpet. Being called in for questioning had already depleted his mental resources. The fear of being caught, the terror of returning to prison . . . and his wife's dead body on the sofa. The answering machine light was blinking. His boss had just fired him.

He had lost everything.

So, rather than try to overcome the insurmountable ordeal, he placed a noose around his neck and jumped.

CHAPTER 61

Because it was an emergency, Justine Philippot freed up a slot in her schedule to see Milo with his godmother and her husband as soon as she could. She had learned about the tragedy, and while she was surprised at Tiphaine's call, she was nonetheless reassured to see her taking such good care of her godson's mental well-being. Exceptional times called for exceptional measures, so Justine suggested a quick chat without Milo initially, followed by long-term therapy for all three of them. Tiphaine agreed gratefully.

"For any child, grieving his parents is a highly individual process," Justine began as Tiphaine and Sylvain sat down. "In Milo's case, it is especially complex since he has lost two other loved ones in recent months too. The fact that his parents took their own lives won't make the healing process any easier. What will happen to him? I mean, where will he go? Who will look after him?"

"He's staying with us for now," Tiphaine said simply. "We're putting together an adoption application."

"That's good. It would be disastrous to uproot him from his surroundings, his neighborhood, his school. All those familiar things are anchoring him right now. It's important for you to realize that although every child experiences the grieving process differently, they nonetheless tend to model themselves on the people closest to them. How you two react to the loss of his parents will be vitally important in the coming weeks. What have you told him?"

"That his parents died in an accident," admitted Sylvain.

"No!" Justine exclaimed bluntly. "You have to tell him the truth! You must explain exactly what happened, in an age-appropriate way, of course, but no lies. It's absolutely vital to his future well-being. He cannot grieve properly based on an untruth."

"How is a little boy his age supposed to understand that both his parents chose to take their own lives?" Tiphaine protested.

"But they did. And the sooner he grasps it, the sooner he can begin the work of healing. He will need plenty of reassurance. Children who have just lost their parents naturally become fearful of their own safety and survival. Who will feed him, who will take him to school? He must be made to feel safe. You have to answer all his questions honestly, reassure him that he is still loved and that you will always be there for him."

"We do that every day," Sylvain assured her.

"And there's more," Justine continued. "Milo will probably be terrified of his own mortality. For a child of his age, violent death seems like a contagious disease, like a cold or flu. And that's doubly the case for Milo because he has now lost four loved ones. He will feel in danger. He may feel sure that his fate is to be like his parents, and you'll have to tread very carefully there. Make sure he understands death is not something you can catch like a disease and that he is a whole person in his own right, not just a carbon copy of his mom and dad."

Tiphaine and Sylvain nodded in agreement.

"Do you think he'll be OK?" asked Tiphaine anxiously.

"With your help, he will be fine. But I won't lie to you. It will be a long uphill journey. He will feel responsible for all the deaths around him. He will feel different from other kids his own age. And if he doesn't get loving support and plenty of attention from the people around him every step of the way, then he could easily end up with major psychological difficulties."

"We'll do whatever it takes," declared Sylvain, squeezing his wife's hand. "We're ready to start therapy with him."

"You'll need it. But with plenty of love, patience, and understanding, he'll be fine."

Justine Philippot studied them, her gaze solemn, then gave a sad, resigned smile. She murmured,

"The little guy is lucky to have you."

CHILD MEDICAL RECORD

AGE 7–8

Your child needs to know you take an interest in their work and you feel you have chosen the best school for their needs. Do not hesitate to go in and talk to their teachers.

> *M. is taking an interest in school again. Therapy with the child psychologist is going well. M. is proving very receptive. He sleeps well. Appetite: room for improvement.*

Your child will be choosing their own friends. Let them meet them outside a school setting and invite them into your home, even if they are noisy or make a mess.

> *M. seems to be getting on well with a girl in his class by the name of Lola. Maybe she's his girlfriend? He doesn't want to talk about it and changes the subject whenever I bring it up.*

> *M. regularly gets invited to birthday parties. He got an all-clear at his last checkup with Dr. Ferreira.*

DOCTOR'S NOTES:

Weight: 52 lbs. Height: 4 ft. 10 in.
A wart on the sole of one foot.
Vitamin D deficiency: take children's vitamin D supplements for four months.
Good general health.

Here ends Barbara Abel's *Mothers' Instinct*.

The first edition of this book was printed and
bound at Lakeside Book Company
in Harrisonburg, Virginia, April 2023.

A NOTE ON THE TYPE

The text of this novel was set in Sabon, a classic and elegant serif typeface designed by the German typographer and book designer Jan Tschichold. Tschichold, who was perhaps best known for his work designing simple and inexpensive layouts for the paperbacks published by Penguin Books in the United Kingdom, was commissioned in the 1960s by a German type foundry to design a modern update of the sixteenth-century font styles created by engraver Claude Garamond. The type was intended to be highly uniform so that it would look the same whether it was set by hand or on a Monotype or Linotype machine, at the request of the German Master Printers' Association. It was named after Jacques Sabon, a French contemporary of Garamond's, and is used today primarily for body text.

HARPERVIA

An imprint dedicated to publishing international voices,
offering readers a chance to encounter other lives and other
points of view via the language of the imagination.